And Then There Were None

Agatha Christie

Level 3

Retold by Izabella Hearn

Series Editors: Andy Hopkins and Jocelyn Potter

Pearson Education Limited
Edinburgh Gate, Harlow,
Essex CM20 2JE, England
and Associated Companies throughout the world.

ISBN: 978-1-4082-6120-0

This edition first published by Pearson Education Ltd 2011

5 7 9 10 8 6 4

Text copyright © Pearson Education Ltd 2011

AGATHA CHRISTIE® *And Then There Were None* Copyright © 2011
Agatha Christie Limited (a Chorion company)
And Then There Were None was first published in 1939.
All rights reserved.
Agatha Christie's signature is a registered trademark of Agatha Christie Limited (a Chorion company).
All rights reserved
Illustrations by Carlos Fonseca

Acknowledgements
The publisher would like to thank the following for their kind permission
to reproduce their photographs:
(Key: b-bottom; c-centre; l-left; r-right; t-top)
Getty Images: Travel Ink 75t; **iStockphoto:** Frank van den Bergh 75b;
Kobal Collection Ltd: Orion 76; **Photolibrary.com:** Britain On View 74
All other images © Pearson Education

Every effort has been made to trace the copyright holders and we apologise in advance for any
unintentional omissions. We would be pleased to insert the appropriate acknowledgement in any
subsequent edition of this publication.

For a complete list of the titles available in the Penguin Active Reading series please go to
www.penguinreaders.com. Alternatively, write to your local Pearson Longman office or to: Penguin Readers
Marketing Department, Pearson Education, Edinburgh Gate, Harlow, Essex CM20 2JE, England.

Contents

1.1 What's the book about?

Look quickly through the pictures in the first few chapters. What do you think? Circle your answers.

1   The story happens in

    a the 1990s.   **b** the 1960s.   **c** the 1930s.

2   A group of people arrive on

    a a beach.   **b** an island.   **c** a mountain.

3   They are in

    a England.   **b** Italy.   **c** South Africa.

4   The people in the group are

    a friends.   **b** relatives.   **c** strangers.

5   Most of them are hoping to have

    a a party.   **b** a holiday.   **c** a business meeting.

6   On the wall of every bedroom, there is

    a a poem.   **b** a picture.   **c** a photo.

7   This is going to be a story about

    a love.   **b** murder.   **c** family life.

1.2 What happens first?

Look at the pictures in Chapters 1 and 2. On which pages are the pictures that these sentences describe? What do you think?

1   At last they could see the house that they were travelling to. ....

2   Mr Justice Wargrave's train travelled quickly through the Devon countryside. ....

3   General Macarthur arrived at Oakbridge Station. ....

4   Vera Claythorne looked carefully at the passenger opposite her. ....

5   Dr Armstrong arrived at the house after the other guests. ....

6   Anthony Marston was driving too fast. ....

7   On the bedroom wall was a children's poem. ....

CHAPTER 1

Journey to Soldier Island

He remembered Soldier Island from when he was a boy. Just a rock, really, covered in birds – about a mile from the coast. A strange place for a house.

Mr Justice Wargrave* looked out of the window of the train. He thought about what he knew, from newspapers, about Soldier Island. After a rich American built a house there, it was bought by a Mr Owen. Or was it? Was it in fact the secret home of Miss Gabrielle Turl, the film star? Or did the mysterious 'Mr L' buy it for his new wife? The newspaper reporters could only guess, but Soldier Island was clearly news!

Mr Justice Wargrave took a letter out of his pocket. The handwriting was difficult, but some words were very clear. The letter was signed by Lady Constance Culmington and it was an invitation to Soldier Island.

Dear Lawrence, ... years since I heard from you ... must come to Soldier Island ... beautiful place ... 12.40 from Paddington ... meet you at Oakbridge ...

He remembered their last meeting, about seven or eight years ago. She was on her way to Italy then, for the sun. Now she had an island! Yes, that made sense. Mr Justice Wargrave smiled and then he slept.

* Mr Justice Wargrave: Mr Wargrave's title, since he became a judge

◆

Vera Claythorne was in a less comfortable part of the train with five other passengers. It was so hot travelling by train today! But she was on her way to the sea. She was lucky to get this job, during her holidays. It was better than looking after children. The letter came from a woman called Una Nancy Owen:

> *... You can start work on August 8ᵗʰ ... I will send someone to meet your train, the 12.40 from Paddington ... I am sending £5 for your journey.*

The address on the letter was Soldier Island, Sticklehaven, Devon. Soldier Island! The place was always in the newspapers! Nobody seemed to know who the owner was.

Vera Claythorne was tired. Her job as a sports teacher was hard work and she would like to work in a better school. But she was lucky to have a job. An unwelcome picture came into her head. Cyril was swimming to the rock and she swam towards him. She was paid to look after him. It was her job. But she knew, all the time, that she was too late. All those mornings, lying on the sand. And Hugo ... Hugo! She must *not* think of Hugo.

She opened her eyes and looked at the man opposite her. He was tall, with a dark face, light-coloured eyes and a hard mouth. *He's been to some interesting parts of the world,* she thought. *He's seen some interesting things.*

Philip Lombard looked back at the girl. *She's pretty,* he thought. *Probably a school teacher – a strong woman. Interesting ... But I must keep my mind on the job. It's all very mysterious.*

'Here's £100. Take it or leave it, Lombard,' were Mr Isaac Morris's words a few weeks' earlier. Lombard needed the money, but asked for more information. 'You will travel to Oakbridge,' said Mr Morris, 'and from there you will travel by boat to Soldier Island. You will work there for a week.'

'It's nothing **illegal**?'

'If anything like that is suggested, you can of course refuse,' Mr Morris said.

Was he smiling? Could he know that the law wasn't always important in Lombard's past?

Lombard smiled now as he remembered some difficult escapes. But he was never caught. He planned to enjoy his time on Soldier Island.

◆

Miss Emily Brent sat up very straight in her seat. It was important to sit well. Politeness was important too. Young people today were rude and lazy, and she had no time for them. When the sun shone, girls took their clothes off. She remembered last year's summer holiday ...

But this year she was going to Soldier Island. She read the letter again, in her mind.

Dear Miss Brent,

I hope you remember me? We met at the Belhaven Hotel in August some years ago.

I am starting my own small hotel on an island in Devon. I shall be very happy to see you there, as my guest. There will be good food and nice people – no loud music. Is August a good month for you? The 8ᵗʰ perhaps?

Yours,

U.N. O—

A free holiday was very welcome, as Emily Brent had little money these days. But the name on the letter was difficult to read. U. N. Olton? Or was it Oliver? Yes, surely she remembered a Mrs Oliver from one of her visits to the Belhaven Hotel.

Soldier Island! It was in the papers all the time – something about a film star – or was it a rich American? Why couldn't she remember more about Mrs – or was it Miss? – Oliver?

◆

illegal /ɪˈliːɡəl/ (adj) that breaks the law

General Macarthur was on a slower train and he was feeling impatient. The place, Soldier Island, really wasn't far, but the journey was so long. Who was this Owen person? He didn't know.

… One or two of your old friends are coming. You can talk about the past. …

Well, he didn't have many friends now, not since that story about him. That was nearly thirty years ago, but people didn't forget. A holiday away from everything, on Soldier Island, was very welcome.

◆

Dr Armstrong was on the road. He was tired. That was the problem with success. After months of waiting for patients in his beautiful but empty rooms, he was now a popular private doctor. He was clever – and lucky too. Women with money liked him and told their friends. His days were full.

general /'dʒenərəl/ (n) an officer with a very high position who gives orders to other soldiers

Dr Armstrong had little free time, so he was pleased about this trip out of London. He was pleased about the large cheque too. These Owens were clearly very rich! The man was worried about his wife's health, the letter said. She didn't want to see a doctor, but the man wanted a report. Luckily, the problem of ten – no, fifteen – years ago was in the past. Dr Armstrong *never* drank now.

Suddenly a fast car passed him, making a terrible noise. Dr Armstrong nearly drove off the road. *Stupid young man!* he thought.

◆

Anthony Marston drove his sports car into the small town of Mere and stopped for a drink. It was hot, but he was excited about his trip to the island. *Who are these Owens?* he thought. *Rich, probably.* His friend Badger was good at finding rich people. Girls, perhaps, and plenty of drink.

Anthony Marston climbed back into his car. A group of young women looked with interest at his tall, handsome body and bright blue eyes. He drove out of the car park very fast. Old men and young boys jumped out of the way.

◆

Mr Blore was sitting in the train from Plymouth, writing a list: *Emily Brent, Vera Claythorne, Dr Armstrong, Anthony Marston, old Justice Wargrave, Philip Lombard, General Macarthur – and the **servants**, Mr and Mrs Rogers.*

That's it, he said to himself. He closed his book and put it back in his pocket. *This job will be easy.* He stood up and looked at himself carefully in the mirror. *I know! I shall be South African. These people know nothing about South Africa and I've read a lot about the place.*

Soldier Island. He remembered Soldier Island from when he was a boy. Just a rock, really, covered in birds – about a mile from the coast. A strange place for a house. A terrible place in bad weather.

An old man opposite him woke up.

'There's a storm coming,' the man said slowly. He was clearly drunk.

'No,' Mr Blore replied. 'It's a lovely day.'

The train stopped at a station and the man stood up and almost fell. Blore helped him to the door.

'The end is near!' the man said as he got out. '*Very* near, young man.'

Sitting down again, Mr Blore thought, *He's nearer the end than I am.*

But in fact, Mr Blore was wrong …

---

servant /ˈsɜːvənt/ (n) a person who does paid work in another person's house

CHAPTER 2

Ten Little Soldier Boys

There was, it seemed, nothing ordinary about Anthony Marston.
Later, a number of people in the group remembered that time.

The little group of people stood outside Oakbridge station. Two taxis were waiting. The driver of the first taxi came towards them.

'Are you for Soldier Island?' he asked.

'Yes,' answered all four people, each looking quickly at the others.

The driver spoke to the judge, the oldest person in the group.

'There are two taxis here, sir. Another guest will arrive on the slow train from Exeter, so one of the taxis will have to wait for about five minutes. Perhaps one of you will wait too and take the second taxi? It will be more comfortable.'

Vera Claythorne looked at the other three and said, 'I'll wait – you go.'

Miss Brent thanked her and got into the first taxi, followed by Mr Justice Wargrave. Philip Lombard introduced himself to Vera Claythorne and offered to wait with her. They moved away to sit on a wall in the sun. Miss Brent and Mr Justice Wargrave enjoyed a short conversation about the weather as their suitcases were piled on top of the taxi. Then they drove away.

'I'm going to Soldier Island to work as Mrs Owen's secretary,' Vera explained to Philip Lombard. 'I've never been here before.' She laughed. 'I haven't even seen my employer yet.'

'Isn't that unusual?' Lombard asked.

'Not really. Her secretary suddenly became ill – and this is a holiday job for me. I work at a girls' school. Is the island very interesting?'

'I don't know,' Lombard said. 'I haven't seen it.'

Should I tell her that I don't know the Owens – or not? he thought. Then they heard a loud noise. 'Ah!' he said quickly. 'Here's the train.'

A tall, older man got off the train. He had grey hair, cut very short, and a small, tidy moustache. He looked like an old soldier. Vera introduced herself and Lombard and the new arrival's eyes rested on Lombard. *A good-looking man,* he thought, *but there's something a little unpleasant about him.*

Vera, Lombard and General Macarthur got into the waiting taxi. They drove along country roads until they arrived at the small village of Sticklehaven.

From there they saw Soldier Island for the first time. Vera was surprised that the island wasn't closer to the coast. And she couldn't see a house – only the dark rock. It wasn't a pretty picture.

Three people were waiting for them in Sticklehaven: Miss Brent, the judge, and a large man who introduced himself as Mr Davis, from Natal, South Africa.

'Let's go then,' he said, and he called a boatman.

The boatman took the group towards a boat that was waiting for them.

'Two more people are coming,' he said. 'But they're arriving by car. I've had orders from Mr Owen. He told me not to wait.'

'That's a very small boat,' said Emily Brent.

'There are a lot of us,' added the judge. 'Are you sure it can carry us all?'

'It can take twice as many,' replied the boatman.

He helped the passengers to climb in.

The boat was ready to leave. Then suddenly they saw a beautiful car speeding down the hill into the village. It looked too fine to be real. In the colours of the evening light, the young driver also looked too perfect, too wonderful to be an ordinary man. There was, it seemed, nothing ordinary about Anthony Marston. Later, a number of people in the group remembered that time.

Fred Narracott, the boatman, was surprised by Mr Owen's guests.

Most of them don't look very rich and important, he thought. *Where are their fine clothes? And what kind of man is this Mr Owen? It's strange that I haven't seen him – or Mrs Owen. But his orders were clear and he's paid for everything. The newspapers talked about a mysterious new owner and they were right.*

Fred looked at his passengers more carefully. Yes, a strange group! The old woman – unmarried and not very pleasant. The man next to her – an old soldier probably. The young girl – pretty, but not special and not Hollywood. The large man – not from the upper classes … a shopkeeper in his younger days perhaps? The thin man with quick eyes – a strange one, *possibly* in the film business? Only one person was, in his opinion, the right kind of guest: the driver of the car (what a car!). He was clearly very rich. But why weren't the others like him? Strange – very strange.

At last they could see the house! It was modern with big windows and a lot of light. An exciting house!

The landing was difficult because of the rocks.

'It's impossible to land here in bad weather,' Fred told the group. 'Sometimes nobody can leave the island for a week or more.'

Fred helped the guests up the steps to the house. At the door of the house a tall, thin, grey-haired man was waiting for them – the manservant, Mr Rogers.

'Come this way please,' he said. Drinks were ready for them and then they could all go to their rooms. Dinner was at 8 o'clock. 'Mr Owen,' he added, 'will not be here until tomorrow.'

Vera followed Mr Rogers's wife into a beautiful bedroom with a big window. There was a door to a bathroom at the side. Perfect!

'Have you got everything you want?' asked Mrs Rogers.

She had black hair pulled back from her pale face. Her strange, light eyes moved all the time. She was frightened of something. What was it?

'Yes, thank you. I'm Mrs Owen's new secretary,' Vera told her. 'You probably know that.'

'No, I don't. I haven't met the Owens yet. My husband and I only came here two days ago,' Mrs Rogers said. 'We're the only servants, looking after eight people – and Mr and Mrs Owen, of course.'

When Mrs Rogers left, Vera walked around the room. She felt a little uncomfortable. There was something strange about all this: no Owens, the pale, frightened Mrs Rogers – and the guests. They were a strange group too.

There was a large, heavy stone clock on a shelf in the bedroom, in the shape of a wild animal. Above that, hanging on the wall, there was a children's poem about ten little soldiers. Vera remembered the poem from years ago. She smiled. Of course! This was Soldier Island!

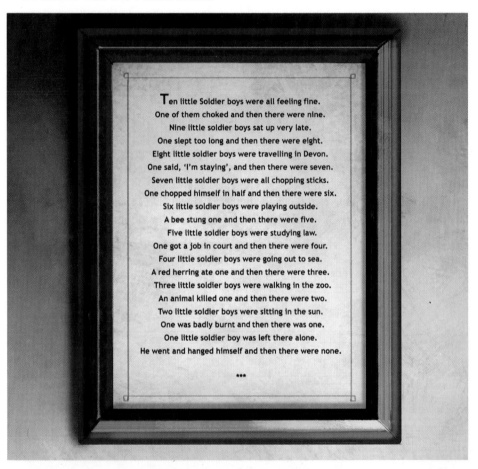

Ten little Soldier boys were all feeling fine.
One of them choked and then there were nine.
Nine little soldier boys sat up very late.
One slept too long and then there were eight.
Eight little soldier boys were travelling in Devon.
One said, 'I'm staying', and then there were seven.
Seven little soldier boys were all chopping sticks.
One chopped himself in half and then there were six.
Six little soldier boys were playing outside.
A bee stung one and then there were five.
Five little soldier boys were studying law.
One got a job in court and then there were four.
Four little soldier boys were going out to sea.
A red herring ate one and then there were three.
Three little soldier boys were walking in the zoo.
An animal killed one and then there were two.
Two little soldier boys were sitting in the sun.
One was badly burnt and then there was one.
One little soldier boy was left there alone.
He went and hanged himself and then there were none.

***

choke /tʃəʊk/ (v) to be unable to take in air. You sometimes *choke* when you eat too fast. You also *choke* when something is tied around your neck.
chop /tʃɒp/ (v) to cut something, like wood, with a heavy tool
bee /biː/ (n) a small black and yellow animal that flies. It takes food from flowers.
sting /stɪŋ/ (v/n) to make a small, painful hole in someone's skin. A *sting* hurts you and makes your skin red.
red herring /red ˈherɪŋ/ (n) something that takes your thoughts away from something important
zoo /zuː/ (n) a place where wild animals are kept. People visit *zoos* to see the animals.
hang /hæŋ/ (v) to tie something tightly around someone's neck and *hang* them from a high place. Finally, they die.

She sat by the window and looked at the sea. So calm today, but sometimes so dangerous. The sea that pulled you down … The sea that could kill …

But no! She refused to think about that!

◆

Dr Armstrong arrived on Soldier Island later that evening. On the journey across the water he asked Fred Narracott about the people who owned the island. But Narracott seemed to know little, or he didn't want to talk.

Dr Armstrong was tired and he needed a holiday. The sea – and rest. There was something restful about an island, he thought. He smiled to himself as he walked up the rocky steps towards the house.

In the garden he saw an old man sitting in a chair. Those pale, clever little eyes … Did he know the man? Of course! It was Wargrave! Sometimes Dr Armstrong was called to his court to talk about questions of medicine. The judge was famous for guiding the court towards his own decisions. He was a hard man. It was strange to meet him here, on the island.

Mr Justice Wargrave remembered the doctor too. Always very careful in his speech, and polite – but stupid, like all expensive London doctors.

'There are drinks inside,' the judge said. 'The Owens aren't here. Very strange. I don't understand this place.' His eyes closed for a minute, then he said suddenly, 'Do you know Constance Culmington?'

'No, sorry,'

'It doesn't matter,' said the judge. 'She has very bad handwriting. I was just thinking – perhaps I'm in the wrong house.'

Dr Armstrong shook his head and went inside.

The judge thought about Constance Culmington, Then his mind turned to the two women in the house – the unpleasant older woman and the girl. He didn't like the girl. Then there was Mrs Rogers, of course. She looked very frightened. But she and her husband clearly worked hard.

Rogers came outside.

'Is Mrs Culmington coming, do you know?' asked the judge.

'No, sir. I don't think so,' answered Rogers.

The judge's face showed surprise, but he said nothing.

◆

Anthony Marston was in his bath, enjoying the hot water after his long drive.

I'm really going to do this, am I? he thought.

But Anthony spent little time thinking. He was a man of action. Warm water – a shave – a drink – dinner.

And then?

◆

Mr Blore was getting ready for dinner. Did he look all right? None of the guests were very polite to him. Did they *know*?

He looked up and noticed the poem on the wall. *That's nice,* he thought. He remembered the island from years ago. And now here he was again, but working this time.

◆

General Macarthur wasn't happy. Everything about the island was strange. He wanted to leave, but that was impossible. There was no boat now. He had to stay. That man Lombard – who was he? There was something unpleasant about him.

◆

Philip Lombard walked silently down the stairs, like a wild animal, and smiled. *A week! What fun!*

◆

Emily Brent was in her bedroom, reading her Bible:

The Day of Judgement will come. Then men will pay for their crimes …

2.1 Were you right?

Look back at your answers to the activities on page iv. Then complete these sentences.

In the ¹ .... , a group of people arrive on an ² .... off the coast of ³ .... They have travelled there by ⁴ .... or by car, and then by boat. Most of them are the ⁵ .... of Mr or Mrs Owen. Some of them are there for ⁶ .... , not for a holiday. But ⁷ .... of them can be sure that they have met the Owens. In each bedroom there is a ⁸ .... hanging on the wall. The poem is about the deaths of ten little ⁹ .... Some of the guests also seem to have death on their minds ...

2.2 What more did you learn?

1 Who's who? Write the names.

Mr and Mrs Rogers	Philip Lombard	General Macarthur
Mr Justice Wargrave	Anthony Marston	Mr Blore
Vera Claythorne	Dr Armstrong	Emily Brent

a An unpleasant old woman full of strong
opinions about other people. ....

b A good-looking but unpleasant man, hoping
for fun. ....

c A young schoolteacher, employed as secretary
to Mrs Owen. ....

d A busy and successful private doctor, asked for
his opinion of Mrs Owens' health ....

e An old man who was quite a famous judge in
the past. ....

f An older man who is unhappy on the island. ....

g A husband and wife, employed as servants. ....

h A man who is planning to lie to the other
guests. ....

i A tall, handsome and probably very rich young
man. ....

2 Discuss why nobody has met the owners of the island.

.3 Language in use

Read the sentences in the box.
Then make sentences with the
words below.

> It **was bought** by a Mr Owen.
>
> The letter **was signed** by Lady
> Constance Culmington.

The house		prepared		Anthony Marston.
Mr and Mrs Rogers		driven		Fred Narracott.
The fast car	was	met	by	a rich American.
In Sticklehaven, the guests	were	built		the Owens.
At the house, drinks		employed		Mr Rogers.

1 ....

2 ....

3 ....

4 ....

5 ....

.4 What happens next?

Look at the pictures. What do you think is going to happen? Tick (✔) your
answers.

1

a ☐ The guests are going to listen to music.

b ☐ They are going to play their favourite records.

c ☐ A voice is going to accuse them of murder.

2

a ☐ Anthony Marston is going to choke to death.

b ☐ He is going to get drunk.

c ☐ Somebody is going to shoot him.

CHAPTER 3

The Voice

'What's happening here? What kind of joke was that?' said General Macarthur in a shaky voice. He suddenly looked ten years older.

Dinner was coming to an end. Everyone was feeling a little happier after the good food and excellent wine. Mr Justice Wargrave was being amusing, and Dr Armstrong and Anthony Marston were listening to him. Miss Brent and General Macarthur discovered that they knew some of the same people. Vera Claythorne was asking Mr Davis about South Africa. Lombard listened while he studied the others.

Suddenly Anthony Marston noticed the ten little soldiers standing on a round glass plate in the centre of the table.

'Soldiers! Soldier Island, of course,' he said.

Vera looked at them carefully.

'What fun!' she said. 'They're the soldier boys from the poem, probably. I've got the poem in my room.'

'It's in my room too,' said Lombard.

'And mine.' 'And mine,' the others added.

'It's amusing, isn't it?' Vera said.

'We're not children,' the judge disagreed.

Vera and Miss Brent left the men to their drinks and went into the sitting-room. The windows were open onto the garden and they could hear the sea.

'A pleasant sound,' Miss Brent said.

'I hate it,' Vera answered quickly. She went red and then continued, more calmly, 'This place probably isn't pleasant in a storm. Perhaps they close the house in the winter. It can't be easy to find servants.'

'No,' Emily Brent answered. 'Mrs Oliver was lucky to get these two. Mrs Rogers is a good cook.'

'Yes, Mrs *Owen* is a lucky woman,' said Vera, correcting the older woman.

'Owen?' said Emily Brent. 'Did you say Owen? I've never met anyone called Owen …'

She didn't finish her sentence. The door opened and the men joined them. The judge sat down next to Emily Brent and Armstrong sat with Vera. Anthony Marston went to the open window. Blore studied the pictures in the room. General Macarthur pulled at his little white moustache and thought happily about the wonderful dinner. Lombard looked at the magazines that were on the table. Rogers brought coffee. There was a silence – a comfortable silence.

Suddenly, into that silence, came The Voice.

Silence, please!

Everyone looked around. Where was the voice coming from? What was happening?

*You are here, **accused** of these crimes:*

Edward George Armstrong, you played a part in the death of Louisa Mary Clees on 14 March 1925.

Emily Caroline Brent, you played your part in the death of Beatrice Taylor on 5 November 1931.

accuse /əˈkjuːz/ (v) to say that a person has done something wrong

William Henry Blore, as a result of your actions, James Landor died on 10 October 1928.

Vera Elizabeth Claythorne, you killed Cyril Ogilvie Hamilton on 11 August 1935.

Philip Lombard, twenty-one African men lost their lives in East Africa in February 1932 as a result of your actions.

John Gordon Macarthur, on 4 January 1917 you sent your wife's lover, Arthur Richmond, to his death.

Anthony James Marston, you murdered John and Lucy Combes on 14 November last year.

Thomas Rogers and Ethel Rogers, you killed Jennifer Brady on 6 May 1929.

Lawrence John Wargrave, you murdered Edward Seton on 10 June 1930.

Have you anything to say?

The voice stopped.

There was a terrible silence and then a loud crash as Rogers dropped the coffee. At the same time there was a scream outside the room. Lombard moved first. He threw open the door. There, lying on the floor, was Mrs Rogers.

Dr Armstrong lifted her onto the sofa.

'It's nothing serious,' he said. 'She'll be all right in a minute.'

Lombard told Rogers to get her a strong drink. Rogers's face was white and his hands were shaking. He quietly left the room.

'Who was that speaking?' cried Vera. 'Where was he?'

'What's happening here? What kind of a joke was that?' said General Macarthur in a shaky voice. He suddenly looked ten years older. Blore was shaking too. Only Mr Justice Wargrave and Emily Brent seemed calm.

Armstrong was busy with Mrs Rogers. Again, Lombard was the one who acted. 'That voice,' he said. 'Where did it come from?'

He threw open the door to the next room.

'Ah! Here we are!' he said.

Inside the second room was a record player. It was against the wall, close to the sitting room. Lombard moved it and saw two small holes in the wall.

He started to play the record again.

Vera cried, 'Turn it off! It's terrible.'

'It's just a very bad joke,' Dr Armstrong said.

'So you think it's a joke?' the judge said quietly.

'But who turned it on?' asked Anthony Marston.

Rogers returned with a glass of wine for his wife.

'I'll speak to her,' he said. 'Ethel! Stop this! Sit up.' Mrs Rogers looked at him with frightened eyes. 'Stop this now, Ethel,' he repeated coldly.

'You'll be all right now, Mrs Rogers,' said Dr Armstrong kindly.

'It was that voice – that terrible voice,' she said. 'Like a *judgement*.'

'Drink,' the doctor said.

She drank and the colour returned to her face.

'I'm all right now. It was the voice. It frightened me.'

'Of course it did,' said Rogers quickly. 'Me too. Terrible lies!'

Mr Justice Wargrave coughed. 'Who put the record on? Was it you, Rogers?'

Rogers cried, 'I didn't know what it was! I can explain. It was Mr Owen's orders. My wife had to put on the record when I was bringing in the coffee.'

'A very strange story,' said the judge.

'It's true, sir! Honestly! I thought it was a piece of music. It had the name of the music on it – *The Last Goodbye*.'

General Macarthur cried, 'We must do something! This is crazy! Who is this Owen person?'

'Yes, who is he?' said the judge. 'Rogers, first you must get your wife to bed. Then come back here.'

'I'll help you,' said Dr Armstrong, and the two men left the room.

Anthony Marston went to find a drink and came back with a bottle and some glasses.

'I found these ready for us outside,' he said.

He poured strong drinks for General Macarthur, the judge and himself.

Emily Brent preferred a glass of water.

When Dr Armstrong and, a few minutes later, Rogers returned, the room became a court of law. Mr Justice Wargrave began.

'Who is this Mr Owen?' he asked Rogers.

'He owns this place, sir,' replied Rogers, 'but I've never seen him. We've only been here a few days, my wife and I. The place had enough food and everything was in order. We were told in a letter to prepare the rooms. Then I got another letter about the dinner and the coffee, and telling me to put on the record. I've got the letter here, sir.'

The judge took it. Blore moved next to him.

'Can I have a look?' he said. 'Hmmm, it was written on a very popular machine. And ordinary paper. Nothing special.'

Anthony Marston looked over his shoulder.

'He has some unusual first names,' he said. 'Ulick Norman Owen!'

'An interesting point,' the judge said. He looked around the room. 'So what information does each of us have about Owen? We're all his guests – so how did we come here?'

Emily Brent began. 'I received a letter. The name was unclear. It seemed to be from a woman called Ogden or Oliver. She talked about a summer two or three years earlier. I thought I knew her. I'm sure that I don't know a Mr or Mrs Owen.'

She went upstairs to her room and returned with the letter.

The judge read it. 'Miss Claythorne?' Vera explained about her job. 'Marston?' He was there because of a letter from an old friend, now living in Norway. The letter told him to go to the island. 'Dr Armstrong?'

'I was called here – by letter – for professional reasons. The letter gave the name of another doctor who I know.'

'But you haven't seen him for some time?' asked the judge,

'Well, no!' said Dr Armstrong.

'Listen!' Lombard said suddenly. 'I've just thought of something.'

The judge lifted his hand. 'One thing at a time, Mr Lombard. General Macarthur?'

'I had a letter from this man Owen. Some of my old friends were coming here,' he said. 'I haven't kept the letter.'

Lombard was thinking. Should he tell the true story or not? He said, 'I had the same kind of letter about an old friend. I believed it. I haven't got the letter.'

Mr Justice Wargrave turned to Mr Blore. 'This is all very unpleasant and we will talk about the voice on the record later. Now I'm interested in the name William Henry Blore. There is no one here with that name, but there is a Mr Davis and he wasn't on the list. Can you explain that, Mr Davis?'

Blore said angrily, 'My name isn't really Davis. I'll have to tell you that now.'

'I want to add something,' said Lombard. 'Mr Blore, you aren't just using another name. You say you're from Natal, in South Africa. I know South Africa and you've never been there in your life.'

All eyes turned to Blore.

'Explain yourself!' said Marston angrily.

'I'm a detective from Plymouth. Owen asked me to come. He sent me money and asked me to join the party as a guest. I was given a list of your names. My job was to watch you all.'

'Was any reason given?' asked the judge.

'Yes, Mrs Owen's paintings ... Mrs Owen! I don't believe she exists!'

The judge was thinking. 'Ulick Norman Owen – U. N. Owen – UNKNOWN?'

'I don't believe it!' cried Vera 'It's crazy!'

The judge agreed. 'Owen isn't just crazy – he's probably dangerous too.'

CHAPTER 4

The Last Drink

He drank quickly. Too quickly, perhaps. He choked – choked badly.
His face turned purple and he fell to the floor.

There was a short silence. Then the judge's small, clear voice began again. 'Before we continue, I'll explain myself. This letter is, it seems, from an old friend of mine, Constance Culmington. I haven't seen her for years. She went to Asia. This is important because "Unknown" knows a lot about us. He knows that a letter from Constance Culmington is never a surprise to me. He knows about Mr Marston's friend and about Miss Brent's holiday two or three years ago and who she met there. He knows about General Macarthur's old friends. And because he knows about us, he's made some terrible accusations.'

'But it's all lies!' shouted General Macarthur.

'We never did …' Rogers began.

'It's a terrible thing to say,' cried Vera.

'I want to say this,' continued the judge calmly. 'The voice accused me of the murder of Edward Seton. I remember him well. He came to my court in 1930, accused of the murder of an old woman. He was well defended and he didn't look like a criminal type. But I knew that he was a murderer. I knew that he had to die. And that's what the court decided. I did my job, nothing more.'

Armstrong was remembering now. The Edward Seton case! It was the judge's final speech that really sent Seton to prison and to his death. Everyone was surprised but it was all quite correct.

'Did you know Seton before the case?' he asked without thinking.

'No,' answered the judge coldly.

He's lying, thought Armstrong. *I know he's lying.*

Vera Claythorne said shakily, 'I'd like to tell you about that child – Cyril Hamilton. I was looking after him. One day, when I wasn't watching, he swam out to the rocks. I swam after him, but I couldn't get there in time … He **drowned**. It was terrible … The mother was very kind to me. There was nothing that I could do. Why is this man saying these terrible things?'

She started to cry and General Macarthur put his hand on her shoulder.

'Of course it isn't true, my dear. The man's crazy,' said General Macarthur. He continued with difficulty, 'And that story about young Arthur Richmond – *that* isn't true. He was one of my officers. He followed my orders and was killed. It happens in war. And my wife was the best woman in the world.'

As he sat down, General Macarthur pulled at his moustache with a shaking hand.

Lombard spoke. His eyes were amused. 'About those Africans … It's true. We were lost and I saved myself. Some friends and I took all the food and ran.'

General Macarthur couldn't believe it. 'You left your men to die?' he said.

'Not very nice, I know, but it was the only way,' replied Lombard.

Vera lifted her hands from her face and said, 'You left them – to *die!*'

Anthony Marston said slowly, 'I've just remembered. Those two children – John and Lucy Combes. Two children ran out into the road in front of my car near Cambridge. There was nothing that I could do. It was just bad luck … I wasn't able to drive for a year after that. It made my life very difficult.'

Dr Armstrong said, 'Speeding is wrong! Young men like you are a danger!'

'It was just an accident,' replied Anthony.

Rogers spoke nervously. 'The voice told a story about me and Mrs Rogers. It isn't true! My wife and I looked after Miss Brady until she died. There was a storm that night, sir, and the telephone was broken. We couldn't call the doctor. I went to him, but he got there too late. We did everything possible for her.'

'But she left you some money?' asked Blore.

'She did, sir,' replied Rogers, 'and why not?'

'And you, Mr Blore?' asked Lombard. 'Your name was on the list.'

Blore's face turned red. 'Landor, you mean? He and his friends robbed a bank – the London and Commercial.'

'I remember,' Mr Justice Wargrave said. 'You gave the information that sent Landor to prison. You were a police officer then. Landor wasn't a strong man – he died in prison a year later.'

'He was a criminal,' said Blore. 'He was the one who killed the bank employee. It was quite clear.'

drown /draʊn/ (v) to die because you are under the water for too long

Wargrave said slowly, 'You enjoyed some professional success as a result, I believe.'

'Yes,' said Blore, 'I did. But I was only doing my job.'

Lombard laughed. 'Aren't we all perfect – except for me! Tell us about you, doctor, and your little professional mistake? What was it?'

Dr Armstrong smiled and said calmly, 'I really don't understand this. What was the name – Clees? Close? I can't remember a patient with that name. It's a complete mystery to me. Of course, it's a long time since I worked in a hospital. Perhaps it's a patient who died there. People always think the doctor did a bad job.' *Drunk – I was drunk. My hands were shaking, I was nervous – and I killed her. Poor old woman – it was a simple job. Luckily the nurse didn't tell anyone. So who knows about it now, after all these years?*

There was silence in the room. Everyone was looking at Emily Brent.

'I have nothing to say,' she said. 'I don't need to defend myself. I've always acted correctly.'

There was an uncomfortable feeling in the air, but Emily Brent stayed silent.

The judge turned to Rogers. 'Are you sure there's nobody on the island except us?' he asked.

'Yes, sir,' said Rogers.

Wargrave said, 'I don't understand why we're here. In my opinion this person is crazy, and may be dangerous too. I think we should leave this place tonight.'

'There's no boat on the island,' Rogers said. 'Fred Narracott comes every morning. He brings everything we need.'

'Then we shall leave tomorrow,' said Mr Justice Wargrave.

Everyone agreed, except for Marston.

'We should solve the mystery before we go,' he said, lifting his glass, 'Here's to crime!'

He drank quickly. Too quickly, perhaps. He choked – choked badly. His face turned purple and he fell to the floor.

Dr Armstrong jumped up and went to him.

'He's dead!' he said in a low voice.

Nobody could believe it! *Dead?* A handsome young man, strong and healthy.

'He choked – and died?' said General Macarthur. 'Is that possible?'

Dr Armstrong picked up the glass and carefully tasted the drink.

'No. It's **poison**,' he said. He smelt the bottle on the table. 'That's all right,' he said.

'You mean Marston put the poison in the drink *himself*?' Lombard said.

Blore said, 'He killed himself? How strange!'

Vera said slowly, 'He was so full of life. He was … enjoying himself! When he came down the hill in his car, he looked … Oh! I can't explain!'

'Is there any other possibility?' asked Dr Armstrong. 'We all saw him pour his drink from the bottle.'

Slowly, everyone shook their heads.

'Marston wasn't the type of man who kills himself,' said Blore thoughtfully.

'I agree,' Dr Armstrong said.

He and Lombard carried Marston's body to his bedroom and covered him with a sheet. When they came downstairs, the others were standing nervously in a group. It was after midnight, but nobody wanted to go to bed.

Rogers went to check his wife.

'She's sleeping beautifully,' he told the doctor. 'I'll just tidy everything and then I'll go to bed too.'

The others went slowly upstairs. Each of them locked their bedroom door.

◆

In his bedroom, Mr Justice Wargrave was thinking about Edward Seton. Seton was a pleasant-looking man with fair hair and blue eyes. Llewelyn tried to prove too much and Mathews defended him well. It was clear that people liked Seton. They weren't sure that he was really a murderer. But then the judge spoke and

poison /'pɔɪzən/ (n/v) something, for example in food or drink, that can kill you

that made the difference. The judge smiled to himself. *Yes, I did it,* he thought, as he climbed into bed.

◆

Downstairs in the dining-room, Rogers was looking at the little soldiers. *That's strange,* he said to himself. *I was sure there were ten of them.*

◆

General Macarthur couldn't sleep. He couldn't get Arthur Richmond's face out of his mind. Arthur was a good friend. Macarthur was pleased, at first, that Leslie liked him too. Leslie! He could see her now, with her deep grey dancing eyes. Out there in France, in the middle of the fighting, he had her picture with him all the time. And then it happened, exactly as it does in books. The letter in the wrong envelope. Leslie was writing to both of them. She sent him Richmond's letter by mistake. Leslie and Arthur! He said nothing when he returned to his wife. But finally he sent Richmond to his death. It was easy enough and he wasn't sorry. But perhaps his assistant, Armitage, guessed that it wasn't a mistake. He remembered those strange looks. Leslie never knew, but she was never very real to him after that. Then she died.

Now he was living in Devon. At first everything was fine. Later he had a feeling that people were talking about him. Armitage? Did he say something? The general stopped going out and his life was lonely. And now, a hidden voice – and a hidden story. And the others? Surely that lovely young girl wasn't a murderer – and Emily Brent! She was clearly a religious woman. *When will the boat come?* he thought. Suddenly he knew that he didn't want to leave the island.

◆

Vera Claythorne was thinking too. *Hugo, Hugo, you're so near me tonight. Where are you really? Will I ever know?* She remembered Cyril pulling at her hand on the yellow beach. 'I want to swim out to the rocks, Miss Claythorne,' the boy said. 'Why can't I?' That evening, on the beach again, Hugo had his arms around her: 'I want to marry you, Vera, but I'm too poor. After my brother's first child died, there was a possibility of money for me one day. And then Cyril was born and now my brother will leave the money to him. It's bad luck, but he's a lovely child.' Cyril wasn't very strong. The kind of child, perhaps, who didn't have a future … Vera heard his voice again: 'Miss Claythorne, why can't I swim to the rocks?'

Vera got up. She looked at the poem on the wall.
Ten little soldier boys were all feeling fine.
One of them choked and then there were nine.
She thought, *That's like us this evening …*

3.1 Were you right?

Look back at your answers to Activity 2.4. Then answer these questions.

1 Who puts the record on? ....

2 Who gave the orders? ....

3 How many people does the voice accuse? ....

4 How many people hear the voice? ....

5 What is in Anthony Marston's drink? ....

6 Are the guests sure that he killed himself? ....

7 How many soldiers are there on the dining-room table, do you think? ....

3.2 What more did you learn?

1 Who is accused of which crime? Write the numbers.

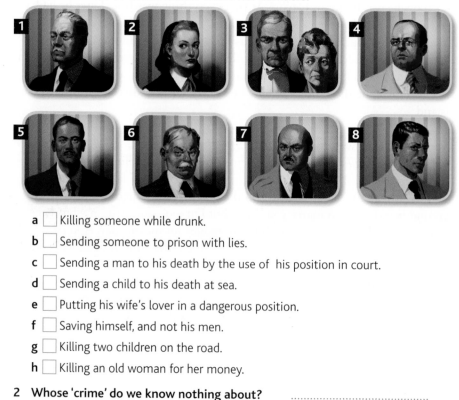

a ☐ Killing someone while drunk.

b ☐ Sending someone to prison with lies.

c ☐ Sending a man to his death by the use of his position in court.

d ☐ Sending a child to his death at sea.

e ☐ Putting his wife's lover in a dangerous position.

f ☐ Saving himself, and not his men.

g ☐ Killing two children on the road.

h ☐ Killing an old woman for her money.

2 Whose 'crime' do we know nothing about? ....

3.3 Language in use

Read the sentences in the box.
Then make one sentence, with _that_ or
who, from the pairs of sentences below.

> Lombard looked at the magazines **that** were on the table.
> He was the one **who** killed the bank employee.

1 There was a silence. It filled the room.

....

....

2 Some guests had letters. They seemed to come from old friends.

....

....

3 Marston hit two children. They ran into the road.

....

....

4 Emily Brent is a strong woman. She refuses to defend herself.

....

....

5 There is no boat on the island. No boat can help them leave.

....

....

3.4 What happens next?

Look at the picture below. How many soldiers are there now? Discuss who will
be the next person to die, and how. What do you think?

CHAPTER 5

A Long Sleep

'You all saw her yesterday. She was accused of murdering that old lady, with her husband. I think that accusation was true.'

Dr Armstrong was dreaming. It was so hot in the hospital. It was difficult to hold the knife. It was very sharp – a good knife if you wanted to murder someone. The woman's body looked different, smaller. He couldn't see her face. Did he have to kill her? Should he ask the nurse? The nurse was watching him. He couldn't ask her. She was looking at him in a strange way. He wanted to see the woman's face. Ah! That was better. A young doctor was uncovering her. It was Emily Brent, of course. He had to kill her. Her eyes were hard and angry. Her mouth was moving. What was she saying? 'In the middle of life we are in death.'

She was laughing now. No, nurse, don't cover her face again! Take it off! It's Anthony Marston! His face is purple, but he's not dead – he's laughing!

Suddenly Dr Armstrong woke up. It was morning and the room was full of light. Someone was shaking him. It was Rogers, with a white face, saying, 'Doctor, doctor!'

Dr Armstrong sat up in bed. 'What is it?' he asked.

'It's my wife, doctor. I can't wake her up. And she doesn't look right to me.'

Dr Armstrong got up quickly and followed Rogers. The woman was lying in bed. Dr Armstrong lifted her cold hand and slowly turned to Rogers.

'Is she, is she …?' Rogers tried to speak.

'Yes, she's dead,' said the doctor.

He looked at the man in front of him and then at the woman in the bed.

'Was it her heart?' asked Rogers.

Dr Armstrong thought before he spoke.

'Did she have any problems with her heart?' he asked.

'No, doctor, nothing.'

'Has she seen her doctor in the last few months?'

'A doctor? We haven't seen a doctor for years. She was never ill,' said Rogers.

'Did she sleep well?' asked Armstrong,

Rogers looked away. 'Well, no,' he replied quietly.

'Did she take any medicine to help her?'

Rogers was surprised. 'No, I don't think so.'

There were a number of bottles in the cupboard, but nothing special.

Rogers said, 'She didn't have anything last night, sir – only what you gave her …'

◆

At nine o'clock everyone was up and ready for breakfast. Vera Claythorne and Philip Lombard walked to the top of the island. There they discovered William Blore, looking for the boat.

Vera smiled. 'Things are usually late in Devon,' she said.

'What do you think of the weather?' asked Lombard.

Blore looked at the sky. 'It looks all right to me,' he said.

'I think there's going to be a storm,' Lombard said.

As they walked back to breakfast, Lombard and Blore talked about Anthony Marston. Why did a man like Marston want to kill himself? It didn't seem possible.

They went into the dining-room.

'Rogers looks ill this morning,' said Emily Brent.

Dr Armstrong was standing by the window.

'Rogers is doing the best he can,' he said. 'He's alone this morning as Mrs Rogers isn't – er – able to work.'

Emily Brent looked at the doctor.

'What's the matter with the woman?' she asked.

'Let's start our breakfast – the eggs will get cold. After that there are things that I want to discuss with you,' said Armstrong.

Plates were filled, and coffee and tea were poured. They talked about news from abroad and the world of sport. Nobody spoke about the island.

When breakfast ended, Dr Armstrong moved his chair back a little.

'I have a sad piece of news. Mrs Rogers is dead. She died in her sleep.'

There were cries of surprise around the table.

'Oh no! That's terrible!' said Vera, 'Two deaths on the island!'

'What happened?' asked Mr Justice Wargrave.

'I'm not sure,' said Armstrong.

'She seemed very nervous,' Vera said. 'Perhaps her heart failed?'

Suddenly Emily Brent's voice filled the room.

'Fear! She died of fear! You all saw her yesterday. She was accused of murdering that old lady, with her husband. I think that accusation was true. She was judged – and then she died!' Everyone looked at Emily Brent in surprise. She looked back at them with shining eyes. 'It's what I believe,' she said.

'My dear lady,' said the judge quietly, 'a court of law is where we judge criminals. Your suggestion is impossible.'

Emily Brent turned away.

Blore said, 'What did she eat and drink before bed last night? A cup of tea? Water?'

'Rogers says that she had nothing,' answered Dr Armstrong.

'Ah!' said Blore 'Rogers *says* that, does he?'

The doctor looked at him and Philip Lombard said, 'So, that's your idea?'

'Why not?' said Blore. 'We all heard that accusation last night. Maybe it was a lie, but maybe not. Maybe it was true. Rogers and his wife killed the old lady and they've felt quite safe and happy about it. Then what happens? First the voice. Then Mrs Rogers falls and her husband is clearly worried. He thinks she's going to say something. She becomes a danger to him. So he puts something in her tea and shuts her mouth forever.'

Armstrong said slowly, 'There was no empty cup by her bed – there was nothing. I looked.'

'Of course there was nothing,' said Blore. 'He washed the cup and put it away!'

There was a silence. Before anyone could speak, Rogers came in. He looked around.

'Is there anything I can get you?' he said.

'What time does the boat usually come?' asked Mr Justice Wargrave.

'Between seven and eight, sir. Sometimes it's a little late. I don't know what Fred Narracott is doing this morning.'

'What's the time now?'

'It's ten to ten, sir.'

Rogers waited. General Macarthur suddenly spoke.

'I'm sorry about your wife, Rogers. The doctor has just told us.'

'Yes, thank you, sir,' said Rogers.

He took an empty plate and left the room. Again there was silence.

General Macarthur went into the garden with Lombard and Blore.

'The boat won't come,' he said quietly. 'We're not going to leave the island. It's the end – the end of everything. It's a good feeling, not to have to continue.'

He turned and walked away.

Dr Armstrong went outside. He saw Lombard and Blore to his left. To his right Wargrave was now walking slowly up and down.

Rogers came quickly out of the house.

'Can I speak to you sir, please?' he said.

Armstrong turned. Rogers's face was a grey green colour. His hands shook.

'What's the matter?' the doctor asked.

Rogers opened the door to the dining-room and they went in.

'Things are happening, sir,' he said. 'Things that I don't understand. You'll think I'm crazy, sir. There were ten of those little soldiers on the table. I know there were ten of them. Last night, when I was cleaning, there were only nine. I thought it was strange. And now, sir, there are only eight! *Only eight ...*'

◆

Emily Brent and Vera Claythorne walked to the top of the island again to watch for the boat. They could see the sea, and the red rock near the village of Sticklehaven, but no boats.

Vera was afraid. *This isn't like me,* she thought to herself angrily. After a few minutes she said, 'I want to get away. I can't understand what's happening. It doesn't make sense.'

Emily Brent said, 'Why did I believe that letter?'

Vera looked at her and asked in a quiet voice, 'Do you really think that Rogers and his wife killed that old lady?'

'Oh yes, I'm sure of it. The man dropped the coffee when he heard the voice. And she was so frightened. *For every crime, there is a punishment.*'

Vera said nervously, 'But, Miss Brent, what about all the other accusations? Are they true too?'

Emily Brent said, 'Mr Lombard left twenty men to die. He told us that. But the judge, of course, was only doing his job. The police officer was too. And *I* didn't do anything wrong. I didn't want to say anything yesterday, not in front of the men.' Vera listened with interest. 'Beatrice Taylor was my servant. Not a nice girl, but I didn't know that then. She was polite and clean and worked hard. I was pleased with her. But some time later I learned that she was a very different type of girl. She was "in trouble", as people say. A baby! I couldn't believe it. She came from a good family. Naturally, she had to leave immediately. I couldn't keep her. Then the girl did something even worse. She killed herself. She threw herself in the river.'

'Weren't you sorry? Did you think her death was the result of your decision?'

'No,' Emily Brent replied.

Vera looked at her. She was a strange old woman – and suddenly she was terrible.

CHAPTER 6

The Search

'A lot of criminals are ordinary people – often quite pleasant.'
'I don't think this one is going to be that kind of killer, Dr Armstrong.'

Dr Armstrong went outside again. Judge Wargrave was sitting in a chair, looking out to sea. Lombard and Blore were smoking but not talking. The doctor wanted to talk to someone, but who? He decided on Lombard.

'Can I speak with you for a minute?'

'Of course.'

The two men walked across the garden.

'Do you think Blore is right about that woman?' Armstrong asked.

'Well, it's possible that Mr and Mrs Rogers *did* murder the old lady,' replied Lombard. 'But how did they do it? Poison?'

'I asked Rogers about Miss Brady this morning. She took medicine for a weak heart. If she wasn't given the medicine … They didn't have to *do* anything.'

Lombard thought for a minute. 'That explains Soldier Island. There are crimes that nobody can punish you for. Old Wargrave, for example – his was a perfectly legal murder. I'm sure he murdered Edward Seton. But he was very clever and did it from his judge's seat. You can't punish him for that.'

A sudden thought passed through Armstrong's mind: *Murder in a hospital. Safe, yes. Completely safe.*

'What do you think about all this?' asked Lombard.

'Let's think about Mrs Rogers's death. Rogers killed her to stop her talking. Or she was frightened and killed herself, like Marston. But I don't believe that Marston, a young man full of life, *did* kill himself. And where did he get the poison from? It's strange. Did he bring it here, or … I know you're thinking it too … *Was Anthony Marston murdered?*'

The two men were silent for a minute.

'And Mrs Rogers?' said Dr Armstrong.

Lombard continued slowly, 'I can't believe that two people have killed themselves. I can believe that Rogers killed his wife, but that doesn't explain Marston's death.'

Armstrong told Lombard about the little soldiers.

'Yes, there *were* ten last night at dinner,' said Lombard. 'And now there are only eight?'

'*Nine little soldier boys sat up very late.*

One slept too long and then there were eight,' said Armstrong.

The two men were silent again.

Lombard said, 'Anthony Marston choked and Mrs Rogers died in her sleep. And there's another type of soldier: the Unknown Soldier. Mr U.N. Owen!'

'I'm glad you agree,' said Armstrong. 'Rogers says that we're the only people on this island. I think he's wrong. He isn't lying – he's frightened. Terribly frightened.'

'Yes, and no boat came this morning. Nobody will come to Soldier Island until Mr Owen has finished his job. But the island is a rock, with very few trees. So we'll soon find him.'

'He'll be dangerous,' said Armstrong.

'I'll be dangerous too when I find him,' Philip Lombard laughed. 'Let's ask Blore to help us. We won't tell the women – or the general or old Wargrave. The three of us can do this.'

Blore agreed to help. 'The business with the ten soldiers – that makes me sure. But there's another possibility. Perhaps Owen isn't doing the killing himself. Perhaps Marston got frightened and poisoned himself. Then Rogers was worried and killed his wife. Was that all part of Owen's plan?'

'But the poison?' Armstrong said.

'Yes, you're right' Blore agreed. 'That isn't something that you usually carry with you. But how did it get into his drink?'

'I've been thinking about that,' said Lombard. 'Marston had more than one drink that night. Between the drinks, his glass was on a table. I think it was on the table by the window. The window was open. Perhaps someone put the poison in and we didn't notice.'

'That's true,' said Armstrong slowly. 'We were all busy thinking about other things. And we were moving around the room.'

'Right,' said Blore. 'Has anyone got a gun?'

Lombard said, 'Yes, I've got one. I usually carry it with me.'

Blore's face showed his surprise. 'Oh,' he said. 'Well, if there's a murderer on the island, he'll have a gun too, or a knife.'

'Perhaps,' said Armstrong. 'But a lot of criminals are ordinary people – often quite pleasant.'

Blore said, 'I don't think this one is going to be that kind of killer, Dr Armstrong.'

The three men started their tour of the island. There were few trees and few hiding-places. They worked carefully, from the sea up to the highest rocks, looking for holes in the rock.

They came to the place where General Macarthur sat looking out to sea. He didn't notice them until Blore walked closer to him.

'You've found a quiet place here,' Blore said.

'There's so little time – so little time. Please leave me alone.'

'We're just making a tour of the island,' said Blore. 'We think that someone's hiding on it.'

'You don't understand. Please go away,' the general answered.

Blore joined the others. 'He's crazy,' he said. 'He says there's no time. He wants to be alone.'

The three men finished the search.

Lombard said, 'There's a storm coming. It's a pity that we can't see the village from here. We need to send a message.'

Blore said, 'Yes, light a fire, perhaps.'

Lombard said, 'The villagers were probably told not to take any notice of anything on the island. They probably think that we're playing a game or something. It's easier to believe than the reality. Nobody's going to believe that Mr Owen wants to murder all his guests.'

Looking down a steep rock to the sea below, he had an idea. 'Is it possible for someone to climb down here? Perhaps there's a hole in the side of the rock. If you get me a **rope**, I'll go down there.'

Blore went towards the house to find a rope.

The wind was getting stronger. Armstrong was thinking about Macarthur. How crazy was the old general?

◆

Vera felt nervous all morning. She didn't want to be near Emily Brent. She walked slowly to the far end of the island. There she saw an old man looking out to sea.

General Macarthur turned his head.

'Ah, it's you!' he said. 'This is a good place to wait'.

'To wait? What are you waiting for?' asked Vera.

'The end. I think you know that, don't you?' said General Macarthur. 'It's true, isn't it? We are all waiting for the end. We aren't going to leave this island. I loved Leslie, my wife. I loved her very much. So I sent Richmond to his death. It was murder. I didn't think so then, but now … Did Leslie know? I'm not sure. It was impossible to talk to her. And then she died and I was alone … I shall welcome the end. You will too, believe me.'

'I don't know what you mean!' cried Vera.

'I *know*, my child, I *know* …' said General Macarthur quietly.

◆

Blore returned with a rope.

'Where's Lombard?' he asked Armstrong.

'He'll be back soon. Listen, Blore, I'm worried. Old Macarthur, how crazy is he?' Armstrong looked at Blore.

'Oh no, I don't think that's possible …'

'You're probably right. Look – here comes Lombard.'

Armstrong and Blore helped him tie the rope. Then they watched him climb down.

Blore turned to Armstrong and said, 'Did you bring a gun with you?'

'No, of course not!' answered Armstrong.

'*So why did Mr Lombard?*' said Blore.

A few minutes later Lombard climbed back up.

'He's in the house – or nowhere,' he said.

---

rope /rəʊp/ (n) something long and strong. You can tie things together with a *rope*, or climb up and down it.

4.1 Were you right?

Think back to your discussion in Activity 3.4. Then complete these sentences.

> ¹........................... dies next, in her ²........................... . ³..........................., of course is already dead. After breakfast, Rogers notices that ⁴................... little soldier boys are missing from the dining-room table. Now there are only ⁵................... .

4.2 What more did you learn?

1 Are these sentences true (T) or untrue (U)?

a Mrs Rogers had heart problems.   ....

b Emily Brent thinks that she died of fear.   ....

c Blore thinks that Mrs Rogers killed herself.   ....

d The boat doesn't arrive.   ....

e Emily Brent tells Vera her story.   ....

f Three of the guests search for Mr Owen.   ....

g Blore has a gun.   ....

2 Who is speaking? Write the names. Then discuss with another student what each person is talking about.

a 'A court of law is where we judge criminals.'   ....

b 'There was no empty cup by her bed.'   ....

c 'Naturally, she had to leave immediately.'   ....

d 'There are crimes that nobody can punish you for.'   ....

e 'There's another possibility. Perhaps Owen isn't doing the killing himself.'   ....

f 'There's so little time – so little time. Please leave me alone.'   ....

g 'They probably think that we're playing a game or something. It's easier to believe than the reality.'   ....

4.3 **Language in use**

Read the sentences in the box. Then
make sentences with these words,
using present perfect verb forms.

> You**'ve found** a quiet place here.
> I can't believe that two people
> **have killed** themselves.

1 Why / Mrs Rogers /die?
   Why has Mrs Rogers died?

2 Why / Fred Narracott / not come?

3 The general / be / unhappy for a long time.

4 In her own opinion, Miss Brent / not do /anything wrong.

5 Who / take / the little soldiers?

6 Mr Owen / not finish / his job yet.

7 The three men / not find / him on the island.

4.4 **What happens next?**

What do you think Emily Brent is writing? Who is going to die next?
Does Emily Brent know the name of the murderer? Do you? Make notes.

Notes

CHAPTER 7

Another Murder!

'Mr Owen believes that we're all murderers. He's brought us here because the law can't touch us. Now we need to save our lives.'

The three men finished searching the island – and the house. Nobody.

'We were wrong!' Lombard said slowly. 'Two people died, one after the other, and we started imagining things.'

'I'm a doctor,' Armstrong replied. 'Marston wasn't the type of person who kills himself. And his death wasn't an accident.'

'Is it possible that Mrs Rogers's death was an accident?' said Blore. His red face grew redder. 'You gave her some medicine last night, doctor, to help her sleep. Perhaps you gave her too much …?'

'Of course not! Are you accusing me of killing her?' said Dr Armstrong angrily.

'People make mistakes,' Blore said.

'Doctors don't make mistakes like that,' said Armstrong coldly.

'If the accusations on the record are true, it's happened before,' said Blore slowly.

Armstrong's face went white.

'What about you?' Lombard said quickly to Blore. 'Telling lies in court!'

Blore was angry now. 'I did not! And there's one thing that I want to know about you, Lombard. Why did you bring a gun with you?'

Lombard smiled. 'Maybe you're not so stupid, Blore. I was paid to come here by a Mr Morris. He told me to keep my eyes open. He didn't say any more than that. I needed the money, so I came. And I brought my gun.'

'Why didn't you tell us this last night?' asked Blore.

'I thought the deaths were the reason for my invitation,' answered Lombard. 'But now I'm not so sure. I think we're all here for the same reason. We're all in danger. We're here because Mr Owen has a plan for us. But where *is* Owen?'

They heard the call to lunch and went towards the dining-room.

'I hope you'll enjoy the lunch,' Rogers said. 'There are potatoes and cold meat. We have plenty of food.' Then he added, 'But I'm worried that Fred Narracott hasn't come this morning. It's very strange.'

Miss Brent arrived, carrying a bag of grey wool.

'The weather's changing,' she said. 'The wind's quite strong and the sea's getting rough.'

Mr Justice Wargrave came in, followed by Vera Claythorne.

'General Macarthur is still sitting by the sea,' Vera said. 'He probably doesn't know that it's lunch time. He's acting a little strangely today.'

Dr Armstrong went to get him. The others started to eat.

When Rogers was picking up empty plates, he suddenly stopped. 'Someone's running!' he said in a frightened voice.

They all knew. And then Dr Armstrong stood at the door.

'General Macarthur! He's dead!' he said.

Each of the seven people looked at the others. Nobody knew what to say.

They brought the old man's body inside just before the rain started. Blore and Armstrong took the body upstairs.

Vera returned to the dining-room. She was looking at the table as Rogers came in behind her.

'You're right, Rogers,' Vera said. 'Look – *there are only seven!*'

Armstrong examined the body, then returned to the sitting-room.

'*This* wasn't an accident,' he said. 'Somebody hit him on the back of the head. I don't know what they used.'

Mr Justice Wargrave spoke. 'So now we can be sure. This morning I was watching you men. It was clear that you were looking for someone. So you also thought that the deaths weren't an accident. Nobody has killed themselves. Mr Owen believes that we're all murderers. He's brought us here because the law can't touch us. Now we need to save our lives. I too believe there's nobody on the island except the seven of us. So it's perfectly clear. Mr Owen is one of us.'

Vera started to cry.

'We must look at the facts,' Mr Justice Wargrave continued. 'One of us is a very dangerous little soldier boy! Do you all agree?'

Everyone agreed.

Blore said nervously, 'Lombard's got a gun. He didn't tell us that last night.'

Lombard repeated his story.

Blore said, 'How do we know that's true? How can we know *what* to believe?'

'That's the problem,' said the judge. 'We can't! So who clearly *didn't* murder General Macarthur?'

'Well, I'm a well-known professional man,' said Armstrong. 'The idea that *I*...'

Mr Justice Wargrave said, 'I too am well known. But doctors have turned to crime before – and policemen. Your profession is no excuse.'

Lombard said, 'We'll leave the women out of this, of course.'

'Do you think that women can't be criminals?' asked the judge. 'Dr Armstrong, is it possible that a *woman* hit General Macarthur on the back of the head?'

'It's perfectly possible,' answered Dr Armstrong.

Mr Justice Wargrave said, 'And a poisoner doesn't need to be strong.'

'You're crazy!' cried Vera.

'My dear young lady, I'm not accusing you. I hope, Miss Brent, that you don't think so either.'

'Of course I can't take the life of another person,' Miss Brent answered. 'But we're all strangers. I understand that you can't know that. We're all possible murderers.'

'Well, it isn't Rogers,' said Lombard. 'He's not clever enough and his wife was one of the **victims**.'

'I've known a number of people who murdered their wives,' said the judge. 'We don't know that Rogers and his wife really murdered their employer. Perhaps he told a lie on the record so there was a crime for each of us.'

'All right.' said Lombard. 'One of us – of all seven of us – is the killer.'

'There can be no exceptions. We must look at the facts,' said the judge. 'Who had the possibility of killing all three victims?'

'This is more interesting,' said Blore, and his eyes shone. 'When Marston was poisoned, we were all there – except perhaps Rogers. Mrs Rogers? It was easy for the doctor or for Mr Rogers to poison *her*!'

Dr Armstrong jumped up, shaking. 'I gave the woman an ordinary ...'

'Dr Armstrong.' A small, cold voice stopped him. 'Naturally you're angry,

victim /'vɪktɪm/ (n) someone who suffers because of another person's actions

but we're looking at the facts. Are there any other possible poisoners? Let's think. Marston and Lombard lifted her onto the sofa. Rogers went to get the drink. Most of us went to the next room to find out about the voice. Miss Brent was alone in the room with Mrs Rogers.'

Emily Brent put down her wool. 'Oh, this is stupid!'

'But these are the facts,' continued the judge. 'Then Rogers came in with the drink and gave it to her. Dr Armstrong and her husband helped her upstairs to bed and the doctor gave her some medicine. Left upstairs, Mrs Rogers slept. But if somebody went up with more medicine "on the doctor's orders", she probably took it …'

'Yes, it's possible,' said Armstrong.

'So we're all still possible killers,' said Blore.

'Let's think about the time of General Macarthur's murder,' the judge continued. 'I spent the morning in the garden.'

'I was with Mr Lombard and Dr Armstrong all morning,' said Blore.

Armstrong added, 'Yes, but you went to get the rope. You took a long time.'

Blore's face went red. 'What do you mean, Armstrong?'

Mr Justice Wargrave looked at Armstrong and asked, 'Were you and Mr Lombard together all the time?'

'Yes, except for a minute or two when Lombard was looking for a way down the rock. He wasn't gone for long enough to murder anyone.'

'A minute or two?' said the judge. 'Did you have a watch? How do you know that it wasn't longer?'

He turned to Emily Brent.

'I walked to the top of the island with Vera Claythorne,' she said. 'Then I sat outside in the sun until lunchtime. I was around the corner, out of the wind, so I didn't see anyone.'

'And you, Miss Claythorne?' asked the judge.

'I was with Miss Brent and then I talked to General Macarthur. It was about an hour before lunch, I think. He seemed very strange. He was "waiting for the end". He frightened me … Then I went back to the house, but I went out again. I was feeling nervous.'

'So that leaves Rogers,' said the judge.

Rogers joined them in the sitting-room. He had little to tell. Lunch preparations kept him busy all morning. But he was sure that there were eight soldier boys before lunch.

'Well,' said the judge, 'until now the murderer's job has been easy. Now we must keep our eyes and ears open at all times. We must all be very careful. We are all in danger – nobody is safe.'

CHAPTER 8

A Late Breakfast

'We must get out of here,' Dr Armstrong said angrily.
'That isn't going to happen,' said Mr Justice Wargrave.

'Do you believe it?' Vera asked. She was in the sitting-room with Philip Lombard. Outside it was raining hard.

'It's difficult to say,' said Lombard. 'But I'm sure there have been three murders. There's no question now of accidents.'

'It is like a terrible dream. Who do you think it is?' asked Vera.

'You mean except for you and me?' Lombard laughed. 'You look like a sensible girl. What do you think?'

'Well, I can't imagine that you're a murderer!'

'You're right! Well, if it isn't you or me, there are five other people. I choose Wargrave. He was a judge, playing with people's lives. It's probably difficult to stop doing that. And you?'

'Dr Armstrong,' she said. 'You see, two of the deaths have been poison. And doctors have so much work – it's hard. Sometimes, they probably go crazy. Also, the doctor went to get the general. Perhaps he killed him then? We're not doctors. We don't know when the general died.'

'That's a very clever idea,' Lombard agreed.

◆

'Who is it, Mr Blore? That is what I want to know. Who is it?' Rogers said urgently. 'If it's one of us, which one? You've got an idea, haven't you?'

'Perhaps,' said Blore, 'but I'm not sure. What do you think, Rogers?'

'I don't know. That's what's so frightening …'

◆

'We must get out of here,' Dr Armstrong said angrily.

'That isn't going to happen,' said Mr Justice Wargrave. 'I don't think a boat will be able to reach us for twenty-four hours. There's too much wind. And, of course, they don't know what's happening. But remember – the three victims weren't prepared. We are.'

'But will the murderer kill us in our beds?' replied the doctor. 'What can we do?'

'There are a number of things that we can do,' said Wargrave slowly. 'I can't prove it, but there's one person …'

'I don't understand. Do you mean you *know*?' cried Dr Armstrong.

'Yes, I think so,' said the judge.

◆

Miss Brent was in her bedroom. She was sitting at the window reading her Bible. She put it down and picked up her little black notebook. She opened it and began to write:

A terrible thing has happened. General Macarthur is dead. He was murdered! After lunch the judge made a very interesting speech. He thinks that one of us is the murderer. I believe that he is right. Which one of us is it? They are all asking themselves that. Only I know ...

She sat for some time without moving. Then, with a shaking hand, she wrote:

THE MURDERER'S NAME IS BEATRICE TAYLOR

Her eyes closed. Suddenly they opened again. She looked down at her notebook. Angrily she put a line through the last sentence. *Did I write that?* she thought. *Did I? Beatrice is dead! Am I going crazy?*

♦

Later, everyone was in the sitting-room, listening to the storm. They were all watching each other nervously. When Rogers brought in the tea, they jumped. He closed the **curtains** and turned on the lights. The room looked brighter.

Vera said, 'Will you pour the tea, Miss Brent?'

'No, you do it, dear,' she said. 'The pot is too heavy for me. And I've lost some of my grey wool. I don't know where it is.'

curtains /ˈkɜːtnz/ (n pl) pieces of cloth that cover a window

Vera moved to the tea table and poured the tea. They sat drinking. Everyone felt calmer. Then Rogers returned.

'Has anyone seen the bathroom curtain – the dark red one?' he asked. 'It was there this morning and now it's gone.'

Nobody answered.

'This is crazy!' Blore said. 'But everything is crazy! It doesn't matter. Forget it. You can't kill someone with a curtain!'

Dinner came, was eaten and was cleared away. At nine o'clock, Emily Brent and Vera went to bed. Lombard and Blore went up with them and heard them lock their doors. They joined the others downstairs, but an hour later all four men went to bed too. They also locked their doors.

Rogers came out of the dining-room and watched them go up. He heard the sound of the four locks. Then he went back to the dining-room. Everything was ready for the morning. He stopped to look at the seven little soldier boys.

Rogers had an idea. He locked the dining-room doors and put the key in his pocket. Then he hurried into his new bedroom. There was only one hiding-place there, a big cupboard. He went inside, then locked that door.

No more little soldier boy games tonight! he thought.

◆

Philip Lombard woke early, as he always did. He listened to the wind, then slept again until half past nine. He sat up. *It is time to do something*, he thought. But at twenty-five to ten he was knocking on Blore's door.

'What's the matter?' Blore said.

'It's twenty-five to ten,' said Lombard, 'and Rogers is missing. He isn't in his room – or anywhere.'

'Where can he be?' said Blore. 'Let's see if the others know.'

They found Dr Armstrong nearly dressed. Justice Wargrave was still asleep.

Vera was dressed, but Emily Brent's room was empty. Rogers's room was empty, but his bed wasn't made and the soap was wet.

Lombard said, 'Let's stay together until we find him.'

They arrived downstairs as Emily Brent came in through the front door.

'Terrible weather. There won't be a boat today,' she said.

'Miss Brent!' said Blore. 'It's dangerous to walk around the island alone. Don't you understand that?'

'I was very careful,' answered Miss Brent.

'Did you see Rogers anywhere?' asked Blore.

'No. Why?'

The judge joined them.

'The table is ready for breakfast,' he said, 'but there's no food.'
They all moved into the dining-room.
Suddenly Vera cried, 'The soldiers! Look!'

There were only six soldier boys in the middle of the table.
They found Rogers outside a short time later, with a deep cut in the back of his head.

'It's perfectly clear,' said Armstrong. 'Rogers was chopping the wood when someone came up behind him.'

Mr Justice Wargrave asked, 'Was it someone who was very strong?'

'No,' replied Dr Armstrong. 'A woman is a possibility – a crazy one!'

Vera Claythorne started laughing loudly. 'Do they keep bees on the island? Don't look at me like that! Bees! Don't you understand? The poem. It's on your bedroom walls, for you to study.

'*Seven little soldier boys were chopping up sticks.*
One chopped himself in half and then there were six.
Six little soldier boys were playing outside.
A bee stung one and then there were five.

'That's why I'm asking. Isn't it funny?'

Vera was still laughing. Dr Armstrong moved towards her and hit her across the face. She stopped.

'Thank you. I'm all right now,' she said in a calmer voice.

◆

'I remember a similar story years ago,' Blore said later to Lombard. 'In the United States. An old man and his wife were both murdered. The daughter was so calm and they couldn't prove anything. But I think she did it. That girl, laughing like that, it's natural. But Miss Brent? She sits in her room reading her Bible. A lot of these old ladies are quite crazy, you know. And she was outside, wasn't she? Looking at the sea. Why wasn't she too frightened to go out? Because she had nothing to be frightened of. *She's* the murderer.'

'That's interesting,' said Lombard. 'So you don't think it was me.'

'I did at first,' said Blore. 'Your story was a bit strange and you had the gun ... But now I don't think so. I hope you feel the same about me.'

'Perhaps I'm wrong,' said Lombard. 'But if you're a criminal, you're an excellent actor. I'd like to know, Blore – did you really lie in court?'

'All right,' said Blore. 'This is the true story. Landor wasn't a criminal and I knew it. But I wasn't making much money. After Landor went to prison, I got a better job, more money ... It was bad luck that he died in prison.'

'Bad luck for you or for him?'

'What do you mean?' asked Blore.

'Well, as a result, you'll probably be dead soon too.'

'No, not me. I'm really careful,' said Blore angrily. 'And you?'

Lombard suddenly looked dangerous. 'I think I'll escape from this. I won't say any more now, but I think so.'

◆

Vera was preparing the breakfast. *Why did I do that?* she thought. *I'm usually so calm. 'Miss Claythorne was wonderful,' they all said. 'She started swimming after Cyril ...'* Everybody was proud of her. Everybody except Hugo – he just looked at her ... Where was he now? What was he doing? Was he married?

'Vera!' said Emily Brent. 'The eggs!'

'Oh, sorry, Miss Brent.' Vera put the eggs on her plate.

'You're very calm, Miss Brent,' she said. 'Aren't you afraid of dying?'

'I'm not going to die!' Miss Brent said. Some people thought so little of death that they took their own lives. Beatrice Taylor ...

Six people were having breakfast. 'Would you like the last egg? More coffee? Can I cut you some bread?' It seemed that there was nothing out of the ordinary. But they were all thinking: *Who's next? What's next? Will it work? It's crazy – everything is crazy! Looking at her, I can't believe it! Wool disappearing, curtains disappearing. It doesn't make sense. Six little soldier boys, only six. How many little soldier boys will there be tonight?*

5.1 Were you right?

1 Look back at your answers to Activity 4.4. Then complete these sentences from Emily Brent's notebook before checking them on page 44.

> A terrible thing has happened.
> a .... is dead. He was murdered!
> After lunch b ....
> made a very interesting speech. He thinks that one of us is
> c .... I believe that he is right. Which one of us is it? Only I know ...
>   THE MURDERER'S NAME IS
> d ....

2 What do you think she wrote the next day? Complete these sentences.

> This morning, I went for a
> a .... When I returned, the other guests were waiting for breakfast. But there was no b .... on the table and we could not find c .... When we found him, he was d ....
> What is happening?

5.2 What more did you learn?

How did they die? Write the correct letter.

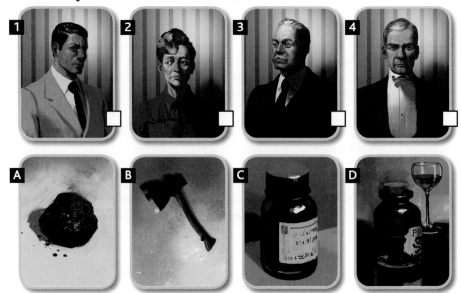

5.3 Language in use

Read the sentences in the box.
Then circle the correct words in the
sentences below.

> **Nobody** knew what to say.
> **Everyone** agreed.

1 They searched the island, but there was *nobody / anybody* there.

2 They were all hungry and *everyone / someone* ate quickly.

3 *Anyone's / Someone's* running!

4 She didn't see *anyone / someone* on the hill.

5 He called *someone / everyone* into the kitchen and spoke to them.

6 Didn't you see *nobody / anybody* in the house?

5.4 What happens next?

There are now six 'guests' on the island. Read these lines from the poem. What
do you think is going to happen? Who to? Talk to other students and make
notes.

Six little soldier boys were playing outside.

A bee stung one and then there were five.

Five little soldier boys were studying law.

One got a job in court and then there were four.

Four little soldier boys were going out to sea.

A red herring ate one and then there were three.

Notes

CHAPTER 9

And Then There Were Four

Vera screamed. She screamed and screamed. Then she heard footsteps, running up the stairs. She fell to the floor.

After breakfast, Mr Justice Wargrave suggested a meeting in the sitting-room in half an hour. Everybody agreed and then began to clear away the breakfast plates.

Miss Brent was feeling unwell.

'I can give you something,' offered Dr Armstrong.

'No!' said Miss Brent. The doctor's face turned white. 'I don't want to take anything. I'll sit here quietly until it passes.'

Emily Brent was left alone in the dining-room. She felt sleepy. Suddenly she heard a sound. *It's like a bee,* she thought. Then she saw it, on the window. *Vera Claythorne was talking about bees earlier,* she remembered.

There was somebody in the room, behind her. *Beatrice Taylor, back from the river.* She wanted to turn her head, but she couldn't. She wanted to call out, but she couldn't. She heard the sound of slow, wet footsteps. The footsteps of the drowned girl ... She could smell something wet. She could hear the bee ... And then she felt it – a bee sting on the side of her neck ...

◆

In the sitting-room, everyone was waiting for Emily Brent. Vera Claythorne offered to get her. But she sat down again as Blore started to speak.

'In my opinion, that woman in the dining-room is the one.'

'It's possible,' Dr Armstrong agreed, 'but we can't prove it.'

'She's very strange,' continued Blore. 'Also, she's the only one who didn't give an explanation for the recording.'

Vera spoke. 'That's not quite true. She told me later.' Vera repeated the story of Beatrice Taylor.

Mr Justice Wargrave said, 'I have no trouble believing that. But tell me, Miss Claythorne, was Miss Brent sorry in any way?'

'Oh no!' said Vera.

'A heart of stone,' said Blore.

'It's now five minutes to eleven,' said Mr Justice Wargrave. 'It's time to ask Miss Brent to join us. Dr Armstrong, please watch her carefully when she comes.'

They all went into the dining-room.

Emily Brent was sitting in a chair. From behind, the others noticed nothing unusual. But then they saw her face.

'She's dead!' said Mr Blore.

The small, quiet voice of Justice Wargrave said, 'So she isn't the one!'

Armstrong was looking at the side of her neck when they heard the sound of a bee at the window.

'It wasn't the bee!' he said. 'It was a **hypodermic needle** – of poison. Probably the same poison that killed Marston.'

'But the bee!' cried Vera.

'Our murderer likes to play games with us,' said Lombard, sounding nervous for the first time. 'He's crazy – completely crazy!'

The judge said calmly, 'Did anyone bring a hypodermic needle with them?'

'I did,' said the doctor. 'Most doctors carry one.'

'Where is it now?' asked the judge.

'In my room,' answered Armstrong.

The five of them went upstairs silently. They looked everywhere, but the needle wasn't there.

'Someone took it!' said Dr Armstrong. 'Someone took it,' he repeated weakly.

The judge said, 'There are five of us here. One of us is a murderer. Dr Armstrong, I must ask you – what medicines do you have?'

'Very few. You can see, here in my case. I have no poison.'

'I have something to help me sleep,' said the judge. 'Mr Lombard, you have a gun. I think we should all put our medicines and the gun in a safe place. Then we should search each person and every room.'

Lombard wasn't happy, but he agreed to get the gun from his room. The judge followed him. Lombard opened the cupboard. The gun wasn't there!

hypodermic needle /ˌhaɪpəˈdɜːmɪk ˈniːdl/ (n) a long, sharp tool used by doctors. It is filled with a medicine which is pushed into a patient's body.

The three men searched his room as Vera Claythorne stood outside. Then they searched the rooms of the other men. Each man also took off his clothes. Vera was asked to put on her swimsuit while they searched her room.

Then the judge put all the medicines in a box in a kitchen cupboard. He locked the box and gave the key to Lombard. He locked the cupboard and gave the key to Blore.

'You two are the strongest. It will be difficult to take the keys from you. But we still have a problem. Where is Mr Lombard's gun?'

'I had it last night,' said Lombard.

'So,' said the judge, 'it disappeared this morning, perhaps when we were looking for Rogers.'

Blore said, 'I don't know where the gun is. But I can guess where the hypodermic needle is. Follow me.'

They went outside and there, not far from the dining-room window, was the needle. Next to it was a broken little soldier boy.

'I knew it!' said Blore. 'The murderer killed her and then threw the needle out of the window. Then he picked up the soldier boy and threw that out too.'

'Let's look for the gun,' said Vera.

The judge agreed, but added, 'We need to stay together.'

They searched the house very carefully, but with no result. The gun was still missing.

◆

Five people – five frightened people. Each person was frightened of the other four. They were five enemies who all wanted to live.

'We can't sit here doing nothing,' Armstrong said. 'Why don't we light a fire?'

'In this weather?' said Blore. The rain was still heavy and the wind was strong.

Without discussing it, they had a plan. When one person left the sitting-room, the other four stayed there together. Lunch was eaten standing around the kitchen table. And all of them were thinking, *Who is it? Which one?*

At five o'clock, Vera made tea while the others watched. Back in the sitting-room, it was already getting dark. They tried to switch on the lights, but there was no electricity. The storm. Lombard left the room alone and came back with a box of **candles**. He lit five and placed them around the room.

Vera's head was aching, so at twenty past six she decided to go upstairs. She left the room with a candle, shutting the sitting-room door behind her. As she opened her door to her bedroom, she suddenly stopped. *The sea … The smell of the sea at St Tredennick. This is the same smell!* 'Can I swim out to the island, Miss Claythorne?' *If this child dies, Hugo will be rich … Hugo!* Was Hugo waiting for her in the room? Her candle went out and it was dark. She was afraid. *Don't be stupid*, she said to herself. *The others are all downstairs – there's nobody here.* But there *was* somebody in the room … and that smell! Then a cold, wet hand touched her, smelling of the sea.

Vera screamed. She screamed and screamed. Then she heard footsteps, running up the stairs. She fell to the floor.

'Look at that!' she heard someone say.

She opened her eyes. **Seaweed** was hanging down in front of the door, like a wet, drowned hand. She began to laugh – a crazy laugh.

Somebody offered her a drink.

'Where did this come from?' she cried.

'I got it from downstairs,' said Blore.

'I'm not going to drink it!'

'You're right, Vera,' said Lombard.

He found a new bottle, opened it in front of her and poured her a glass. She drank it and the colour came back to her face.

'Well, that's one murder that's failed,' laughed Philip Lombard.

Vera said quietly, 'Do you think so?'

'I'm not sure,' said the doctor.

Carefully he tasted the first drink, but there was nothing wrong with it.

'I didn't touch that drink!' Blore said.

Vera looked around. 'Where's the judge?' she asked.

There was silence.

'That's strange,' said Lombard.

They went downstairs and Armstrong called his name.

'Wargrave, Wargrave, where are you?'

There was no answer. At the door of the sitting-room, Armstrong suddenly stopped. Mr Justice Wargrave was sitting in his chair at the end of the room, with a candle on each side of him. He was dressed in a dark red curtain and grey wool sat on top of his head.

---

candle /ˈkændl/ (n) something that you burn for light
seaweed /ˈsiːwiːd/ (n) a plant that is found in the sea

Dr Armstrong lifted the wool. At the front of his head there was a round, red circle.

'He's dead,' Dr Armstrong said. 'Someone shot him!'

'The gun!' shouted Blore.

'Miss Brent's missing wool – and the missing curtains too!' said Vera, her voice shaking.

Suddenly Philip Lombard laughed.

'Five little soldier boys were studying law.
One got a job in court and then there were four.'

CHAPTER 10

Dr Armstrong Disappears

Blore sat on the side of his bed. His eyes were small and red in his large face.
He was like a wild animal. Six out of ten, *he thought.*

They carried Mr Justice Wargrave up to his room and placed him on the bed.

'What do we do now?' Blore said.

'Have something to eat,' Lombard said. 'We have to eat.'

They went to the kitchen and opened a tin of meat.

'Only four of us now,' Blore said. 'Who'll be next?'

'That was very clever,' Lombard said, 'putting the seaweed in Miss Claythorne's room. While we were running to her room, the murderer was killing the judge. We didn't hear anything because Vera was screaming. And there was the wind. But that isn't going to work next time. He'll have to do something different.'

'Four of us,' Armstrong said, 'and we don't know which …'

'*I* know,' said Blore.

'*I'm* sure too,' said Vera,

'I do know really,' Armstrong said slowly.

'I think I have a very good idea,' said Lombard.

They decided to go up to bed and moved slowly to the door.

'Where is that gun?' Blore asked.

Upstairs, each person stood outside their room. Then each one stepped inside at the same time, locking the door carefully.

◆

Philip Lombard opened the door of his bedroom cupboard. He stood there, looking at the gun that was inside it.

◆

Vera lay in her bed. She didn't want to put out her candle. She was afraid of the dark.

Then she thought suddenly, *Of course! I can stay in this room. Food doesn't matter. I can stay here safely for a day or two, or until help comes.*

She began to think of Cornwall – of Hugo – of Cyril. *'Of course you can swim to the rock, Cyril. Your mother gets so nervous, but tomorrow you can surprise her!'* Hugo planned to be in Newquay the next day. Her plan was perfect. When Hugo returned, the boy was dead. But the look on his face – did he know? He went away soon after that and she never saw him again. She wrote him a letter, but he didn't reply.

Vera remembered the seaweed again – the cold, wet touch on her face.

◆

Blore sat on the side of his bed. His eyes were small and red in his large face. He was like a wild animal. *Six out of ten,* he thought. *William Henry Blore is not going to be the next! But where's the gun?* He worried about that.

Later, he lay on the bed in the dark, remembering the cold, dead face of Mrs Rogers and the ugly purple face of Anthony Marston.

Blore remembered another face. Who was it? Of course – Landor! There was a wife and a child too, a girl of about fourteen. For the first time he thought about them, but then his thoughts went back to the gun. Somebody in the house had it.

Suddenly he heard a noise. Someone was moving in the dark house. Who was it? He stood at the door, listening. The noise didn't come again. He wanted to go out and look, but that was dangerous. And then he heard the sound of someone walking softly and carefully past Lombard and Armstrong's room, and then past his door.

He acted quickly. He picked up a box of matches and the electric bedside light. The light was useful because it was heavy. Without putting on his shoes, he ran quietly to the top of the stairs. Through the window he saw the light of the moon. The sky was clear and there was no wind now.

Suddenly he saw someone leaving through the front door. So now one room was empty!

He knocked on Dr Armstrong's door. There was no answer. He waited a minute and then knocked on Lombard's door.

'Who's there?'

'It's Blore, I don't think Armstrong's in his room. Wait a minute.'

He went to Vera Claythorne's room and knocked.

'Who is it? What's the matter?'

'It's all right,' said Blore. 'Wait a minute. I'll come back.'

He ran back to Lombard's room. Lombard stood there with one hand in his pocket, holding his candle in the other hand.

Blore explained quickly.

'So Armstrong's our man, is he?' said Lombard.

He knocked on Armstrong's door. No answer. Carefully he examined the lock.

'The key is not in the door on the inside. He's locked the door from the outside and taken the key with him. We'll get him!'

He ran to Vera's door.

'We're looking for Armstrong! He's not in his room. Don't open your door – do you understand?' He joined Blore. 'Let's get him!' he said.

'We need to be careful,' said Blore. 'Remember, he's got a gun!'

'You're wrong,' said Lombard, and showed him the gun. 'Someone put it back in my cupboard tonight.'

Blore's face changed.

'Don't be stupid,' said Lombard. 'I'm not going to shoot you. I'm going to catch Armstrong.'

He ran off and Blore followed him.

Vera got up and dressed. She started to write in her notebook. Suddenly she heard a noise. It sounded like a breaking window and it came from downstairs. She listened hard, but the noise didn't come again. Then she heard people moving downstairs, and the sound of voices.

'Vera! Are you all right? Will you let us in?' It was Lombard's voice at her door.

Vera opened the door. 'What's happened?' she asked.

'Armstrong's disappeared!' Lombard said.

'That's not possible,' said Vera. 'He's hiding somewhere!'

'It's true,' said Blore. 'But there's another thing. The dining-room window is broken and there are only three little soldier boys on the table!'

◆

Three people sat eating breakfast in the kitchen. It was a lovely day, after the storm.

'We'll try to send a message with a mirror from the top of the island today,' Lombard said. 'The weather's fine, but the sea's still very rough. A boat won't come until tomorrow.'

'What's happened to Armstrong?' said Blore.

'Well,' said Lombard, 'there are only three little soldier boys left on the dining-room table. Armstrong is probably dead.'

'But where's his body?' asked Vera.

'It's strange,' said Blore. 'Perhaps it's in the sea. I don't know where it is. But I do know one thing. You, Lombard, have got a gun!'

'I told you,' said Lombard angrily. 'I found it in my cupboard. It was the biggest surprise of my life!'

'And you want me to believe that?' said Blore. 'Lock the gun in the cupboard with the medicines. You and I will continue to hold the two keys. That's the only fair thing to do.'

'No,' said Lombard. 'It's my gun and I'm going to keep it.'

'All right,' said Blore. 'Then *you* are Mr Owen.'

'That's crazy!' said Lombard. 'So why didn't I shoot you last night?'

'I don't know,' said Blore. 'You probably had a reason.'

'Oh stop it, you two,' Vera cried. 'Have you forgotten the poem?

Four little soldier boys were going out to sea.

A red herring ate one and then there were three.

'A red herring! Armstrong's not really dead! He just took away the soldier boy because he wanted you to think that. Say what you like. Armstrong is still on the island.'

'Perhaps you're right,' said Lombard thoughtfully.

'I'm sure I'm right. We all searched for the gun and we didn't find it. But it was somewhere,' said Vera. 'He's crazy, don't you understand? The poem thing is crazy! He dressed the judge in those curtains. He killed Rogers when he was chopping wood. He gave Mrs Rogers poison so she slept. There was a bee in the room when Emily Brent died. It's like a child playing a terrible kind of game.'

Blore said, 'Well, he'll have trouble with the next line. There's no zoo on the island.'

'Don't you understand?' said Vera. 'We're acting like animals now and we can't escape. *We're* the zoo!'

6.1 Were you right?

Look back at your answers to Activity 5.4. Then change the <u>underlined</u> words in the sentences below. Write correct sentences.

1 Emily Brent dies in the <u>garden</u>.

....

2 She is killed with a <u>large rock</u>.

....

3 The judge is found in the <u>kitchen</u>.

....

4 <u>A red curtain</u> covers a round, red circle on his head.

....

5 Late at night, Dr Armstrong <u>is found in</u> his room.

....

6 Then there are <u>five</u> little soldier boys left on the table.

....

6.2 What more did you learn?

In which order do these happen? Number the sentences 1–8.

a Medicines are locked away. ....

b The bedrooms are searched. ....

c Blore and Lombard look for Dr Armstrong. ....

d The judge's body is carried to his room. ....

e Emily Brent dies. ....

f Vera Claythorne finds seaweed in her room. ....

g Vera decides that Dr Armstrong is the killer. ....

h Blore hears noises in the night. ....

5.3 Language in use

Look at the sentences in the box on the right. Then complete the sentences below with the correct form of these phrasal verbs.

> She didn't want to **put out** her candle.
>
> He **picked up** a box of matches.

get up	come back	go away	call out	clear away
pick up		let in	put back	throw out

1 They began to .... the breakfast plates.

2 Emily Brent wanted to ...., but she couldn't.

3 The murderer .... the soldier boy and .... that .... too.

4 Lombard left the room alone and .... with a box of candles.

5 Hugo .... soon after that and she never saw him again.

6 Lombard showed him the gun. 'Someone .... it .... in my cupboard tonight.'

7 Vera .... and dressed.

8 'Vera! Are you all right? Will you .... us ....?'

5.4 What happens next?

Discuss these questions with other students and write your answers.

1 How many people are still alive on the island? Name them.

   ....

2 Who is the murderer? ....

3 Why is he/she murdering people?

   ....

4 How many people will be alive on the island at the end of the story? ....

5 Will the police be able to solve the crimes? Why (not)?

   ....

   ....

   ....

   ....

CHAPTER 11

No More Fear

Suddenly a terrible noise shook the ground and they heard a cry from the house.
Philip wanted to go and see. Vera was frightened but she followed.

They spent the morning at the top of the island, trying to send a message to the village across the sea. There was no answer of any kind. The sea was calm now, but there were no boats.

They searched the island again, but found no sign of the missing doctor. Vera looked at the house from where they were standing.

'I feel safer out here,' she said. 'I don't want to go back to the house.'

'We'll have to go inside for the night,' said Blore.

'You'll be safe in your room,' added Lombard.

'It's strange,' Vera said. 'I'm almost happy. I know I'm in danger. But nothing matters. I feel that I can't die.'

Blore was hungry and wanted to go inside for some lunch. Lombard offered to stay with Vera.

'We agreed to stay together,' said Blore.

'I'll come with you then,' Lombard offered.

'No, you won't,' said Blore. 'You'll stay here.'

Lombard laughed. 'So you *are* afraid of me?'

'No, but the house makes me nervous.'

'And you want my gun?' Lombard said. 'Well, you can't have it.'

Blore started walking towards the house. Vera looked after him nervously.

'Don't worry,' said Lombard. 'Armstrong hasn't got a gun and he isn't in the house. I know he's not there.'

'So you think it's Blore?'

'Listen, Vera,' he said. 'You heard Blore's story. It means that *I* can't be the killer. But why can't *he*? How do we know that he really heard someone last night? Perhaps he killed Armstrong hours before that. In my opinion he's the one to be afraid of. What do we know about him? It's possible that he murdered every one of the victims.'

'I still think it's Armstrong,' said Vera. 'Don't you feel, all the time, that someone is watching us? I read a story once about two judges who came to a small town in the United States. They judged people there, and sent them to their deaths, but *they didn't come from this world.*'

'I don't believe in things like that,' said Lombard.

'I'm not sure.'

After a short silence, Lombard said very quietly, 'You're worried. So you did kill that boy. There was a man that you loved. Was that it?'

'Yes, there was a man,' Vera agreed in a
tired voice.

Suddenly a terrible noise shook the ground
and they heard a cry from the house. Philip
wanted to go and see. Vera was frightened but
she followed.

They found Blore lying outside, dead on the
ground. Next to him was a large piece of stone.

Vera realised what it was. 'It's the clock
from my room!' she said. 'It's terribly heavy!'
She looked up. 'Look! The window in my room
is open.' She was silent and then she said, 'The
clock was shaped like a wild animal.'

'Now we know,' Lombard said. 'Armstrong
is hiding somewhere in the house. I'm going to
get him!'

'Don't be stupid!' said Vera. 'It's us now!
We're next. He wants us to look for him.'

'You're right. But I've got this!'

He showed her the gun that he had in his
pocket.

'But don't you realise? Armstrong is crazy,'
said Vera.

After a silence, Lombard said, 'Tonight we must find a place on the top of
the island and sit there until morning. We can't go to sleep.'

They walked along the rocks next to the water. The sun was dropping
towards the west.

Suddenly Philip Lombard said, 'What's that there, on that big rock?'

They walked towards the rock.

'It's clothes!' said Lombard. 'That's a boot. Let's get closer.'

Vera stopped suddenly. 'It's not clothes. It's a man!'

They looked at the face – the terrible, purple, drowned face.

'Oh no!' said Lombard. 'It's Armstrong!'

Minutes passed. Minutes that felt like years. Slowly, very slowly, Vera
Claythorne and Philip Lombard lifted their heads. Each of them looked into the
other's eyes.

Lombard laughed. 'So that's it, is it, Vera?'

Vera said quietly, 'There's nobody on the island. Nobody except us.'

Their eyes met.

Why didn't I see his face clearly before? she thought. *He's like a wild dog with those terrible teeth.*

'So now we know,' said Lombard, his voice sounding dangerous. 'This is the end, you understand. We've come to the end.'

Vera said quietly, 'I understand.' She looked down at the dead man. 'Poor Dr Armstrong.'

'What's this? Pity?'

'Haven't *you* any pity?' she replied.

'I've got no pity for *you*,' he said.

'We must carry him up to the house,' said Vera.

'To join the other victims? No! He can stay here.'

'Well, let's move him out of the reach of the sea.'

With difficulty, they pulled the body away from the water.

'Happy now?' said Lombard.

'Quite,' said Vera.

And then he knew. He put his hand in his pocket, but there was nothing there. Vera was standing in front of him, holding the gun.

Philip Lombard knew that death was very near. But he wasn't giving up.

'Give that gun to me,' he said.

Vera laughed.

'Listen, my dear girl, you must listen ...' And then he jumped, as fast as a wild cat.

Without a thought, Vera shot him. His body crashed heavily to the ground.

Vera came towards him carefully, but there was no danger now. Philip Lombard was dead. Shot through the heart.

At last, that was the end! There was no more fear. She was alone on the island ... Alone with nine dead bodies ... But what did that matter? She was alive! She sat there, perfectly happy. No more fear ...

It was getting dark when Vera finally moved. She was hungry and tired. She wanted to throw herself on her bed and sleep and sleep and sleep. She walked towards the house, went inside and moved towards the dining-room.

There were still three little soldier boys in the middle of the table. She laughed and picked up two of them, throwing them out of the window. She heard them crash on the ground outside. Then she picked up the last little soldier boy and said, 'You can come with me. We've won, my dear. We've won!'

She started walking up the stairs, slowly because her legs were suddenly very tired.

One little soldier boy was left there alone … How did it end? Ah yes, he got married and then there were none. Again, she had a feeling that Hugo was waiting for her upstairs. Something fell from her hand. It was the gun, but she didn't notice. *One little soldier boy was left there alone … How* did it end? She opened the door and stopped suddenly.

There, hanging in front of her, was a rope. Under the rope was a chair to stand on. A chair to kick away …

That was what Hugo wanted! And of course that was the last line of the poem.

He went and hanged himself and then there were none.

The little soldier boy fell from her hand as Vera moved forward. This was the end – in the place where the cold hand touched her … Cyril's hand, of course.

'You can go to the rock, Cyril …'

That was what murder was. It was as easy as that. But you always remembered.

She climbed up on the chair and put the rope around her neck. Hugo was there, watching. She kicked away the chair …

CHAPTER 12

The Mystery Solved

'The men didn't get there until the afternoon of the 12th.
They're sure that nobody left the island before then.'

'It's not possible!' said Thomas Legge of Scotland Yard*.

'I know, sir,' agreed Officer Maine quietly.

'Ten people are dead on an island and there isn't a living person anywhere. It doesn't make sense,' Legge continued. 'Somebody killed them, but who? Is there nothing in the doctor's report to help us?'

'No, sir,' Maine said. 'Wargrave was shot through the head and Lombard through the heart. Mrs Rogers, Miss Brent and Marston were poisoned. Rogers and Macarthur were hit on the head from behind, and Blore from above. Armstrong drowned. Vera Claythorne was hanged.'

'And the people of Sticklehaven? Didn't they notice anything?' Legge asked angrily.

'They know that a Mr Owen bought the island. A Mr Morris – Isaac Morris – did everything for him.'

'And what does he say about all this?'

'He can't say anything sir – he's dead. We think he had a criminal past. We can't prove it because he was a very careful man. He bought Soldier Island, but for Mr Owen. He told the people in Sticklehaven a story about a group of people spending a week on the island as a kind of game. The group needed to be alone, so nobody must go near the island.

'In Sticklehaven, people weren't surprised, sir. Elmer Robson, the American, owned the island before that and he had some very strange parties. I'm sure that the people of the village just accepted it. Fred Narracott took the guests out there. He was surprised that they were all so quiet and ordinary. That's why he finally decided to go to the island. He heard that someone was trying to send a message.'

'When was that exactly?'

'On the 11th. Some boys saw signs, but the weather was bad. The men didn't get there until the afternoon of the 12th. They're sure that nobody left the island before then. The sea was very rough. Also, a lot of people were watching the island by then.'

And the record that they found? Can that help us?'

'A theatre company made it for a Mr U.N. Owen. They were told that it was for a play. I've checked the accusations. The Rogers were the servants of a Miss Brady.

* Scotland Yard: the main building for London's police

She died suddenly. Her doctor says that she wasn't poisoned. Perhaps they didn't help her when she needed it. But he couldn't prove anything. The judge? Well, Seton *was* a murderer. We can be sure of that now, but many people at the time thought differently. The Claythorne girl was looking after the boy who drowned. She tried to save him, but failed. That's all.

'Dr Armstrong did have a patient called Clees. She died while he was her doctor. But he was young then – perhaps he made a mistake. He had no reason to kill her. Emily Brent employed Beatrice Taylor and threw her out. The girl drowned – very sad, but there was no crime. Young Marston always drove too fast and he hit those two children, John and Lucy Combes. His friends defended him in court, he paid the family and he was freed.

'I can't find much about General Macarthur. Arthur Richmond worked for him and died during the war. They were close friends. A lot of officers make mistakes and their men die. Philip Lombard. He hasn't always been on the right side of the law. It's possible that he's murdered people. Blore, of course, was one of us. A clever man – but a dishonest police officer. In my opinion Blore lied in court about Landor.'

Thomas Legge thought about this. 'And Isaac Morris is dead?'

'Yes, he died on the night of August 8th. An accident, perhaps – or not.'

Legge said, 'I can't believe that his death was natural. It's all very strange. Ten people on an island, all dead. We don't know *who* did it, *why* or *how*.'

Maine coughed. 'Well, we can guess *why*. None of these people were punished by the law. Mr Owen decided that that wasn't good enough. He killed all ten people and then disappeared.'

'Unbelievable. So, Maine, what's the explanation?'

'There's only one possible explanation, sir. He was one of the ten. We have the notebooks that Emily Brent and Vera Claythorne left. Wargrave and Blore made some notes too. Their stories are all similar. The deaths happened in this order: Marston, Mrs Rogers, Macarthur, Rogers, Miss Brent, Wargrave. Then we learn from Vera's notebook that Armstrong left the house. Blore and Lombard went after him.

'Blore's last words are: *Armstrong disappeared*. Perhaps Armstrong killed the others and then drowned himself. But the police doctor arrived on the island on the morning of the 13th. He says that the deaths were all thirty-six hours or more before that. And Armstrong's body was in the water for eight to ten hours before the sea brought it back to the beach. So Armstrong was already in the sea some time during the night of the 10th–11th. The doctor thinks that the body arrived on the rocks before high water at about 11 a.m. on the 11th. The water didn't reach that point again until after the storm. But his body was above the reach of the water – so somebody pulled him out. Someone was alive!

'In the early morning of the 11th, this is the picture: Armstrong has disappeared (drowned). That leaves us with three people: Blore, Lombard and Vera Claythorne. Lombard was shot – we found his body down by the sea. Vera was hanged in her bedroom and Blore's body was outside on the ground. Let's think about them one at a time.

'Philip Lombard. Let's imagine that he killed Blore and then Vera Claythorne. Then he went to the sea and shot himself. But who took away his gun?

'We know that Vera Claythorne touched it last. So let's imagine that Vera is the killer. She shot Lombard, took the gun back to the house, threw the clock down on Blore's head and hanged herself. But we found the chair against the wall with the others. *It was moved after she died.* That leaves Blore. Did he shoot Lombard, hang Vera and then pull that heavy clock down onto his own head? I can't believe that. And the Sticklehaven people are sure nobody left the island. *So who killed them all?*'

◆

Letter sent to Scotland Yard from the *Emma Jane* fishing boat

From an early age I enjoyed the idea of killing. But at the same time I had a strong sense of right and wrong, so I studied law. Crime and punishment interested me. I enjoyed watching criminals suffer. Edward Seton was one of them. He looked pleasant, but he was a murderer. I made sure that he was hanged for his crime.

For some years I have known that I wanted to try murder too. Not an ordinary murder, of course, but something wonderful – impossible! I wanted to kill ... But I still felt the importance of right and wrong. Then, suddenly, the idea came to me while I was talking to a doctor. He was telling me about a woman who died. He was sure that she was killed by her servants for her money. They decided not to give her the medicine that she needed. The doctor couldn't prove this, so the servants were never punished.

That was the beginning of my plan. I remembered the poem about ten little soldier boys and I began, secretly, to find my ten victims.

A nurse told me about Dr Armstrong during a stay in hospital. A conversation between two old soldiers gave me General Macarthur. A man returned from South America and told me about the activities there – and in other parts of the world – of Philip Lombard. I found out about Emily Brent and her servant from an angry woman in Majorca. I chose Anthony Marston from a large group of dangerous, unfeeling drivers. I heard discussions between other judges about Blore. Then there was Vera Claythorne. I met Hugo Hamilton while I was crossing the Atlantic. He told me about Vera and the boy. It was hard for him to imagine her as a murderer. But he was sure of it. He was also sure that she did it for <u>him</u>. He needed his brother's money, she thought. She didn't realise that in fact he loved that boy. I needed a tenth victim and I found Morris. He was a criminal who destroyed many people's lives.

By this time I knew that I had some serious health problems. I had little time. But I planned to <u>live</u> before I died! So I bought the island, using Morris. Then I gave him some medicine to help with his stomach ache. He took it happily and died in the night.

My guests arrived on Soldier Island on August 8th. Some of their crimes were worse than others. I decided that those people should die last.

I started with Anthony Marston and Mrs Rogers. He died quickly and she died in her sleep. It was easy to put the poison into Marston's almost-empty glass. When Rogers placed the drink for his wife on a table for a minute, I added a large amount of my own medicine. General Macarthur suffered no pain. He didn't hear me coming up behind him. I chose my time carefully and was successful.

After that I needed someone to work with me. I chose Dr Armstrong. He thought that the killer was Lombard. I agreed. I had, I said, a plan. I killed Rogers on the morning of August 10th and found the dining-room key in his pocket. When his body was discovered, I took the gun from Lombard's room. I knew he had one. Morris told him to bring it.

At breakfast I put something in Miss Brent's coffee. When she was sleepy, I poisoned her with the hypodermic needle. I enjoyed placing the bee in the room - I wanted to stay close to the poem. I had no more poison and the gun was in a safe place. So I suggested a search of the rooms.

Then I told Armstrong my plan. I must seem to be the next victim! Then I could move around the house and watch for the murderer. Armstrong liked the idea. We prepared the curtain, the candles, a little colour for my head, and then we were ready. The plan worked perfectly. Miss Claythorne found the seaweed and screamed. Everybody ran upstairs. I stayed downstairs where, later, they found me. In the candlelight, only Armstrong - the doctor - looked at me closely. After they carried me upstairs to my bed, nobody was interested in my body.

Armstrong and I met outside the house in the middle of the night. We talked and then I pushed him from the rocks into the sea. When I returned to the house, Blore heard me. I went into Armstrong's room, made a noise, then left again. I knew that someone was watching me. Blore and Lombard followed me. I went around the house and climbed in through the dining-room window. Then I went up to my own room and lay down. They did pull the sheet back earlier, when they were searching the house. But they didn't look carefully and they went away. I forgot to say that I returned the gun to Lombard's room. Before that, the gun was in the kitchen, hidden under a pile of boxes. The curtain was under the cover of a dining-room chair and Miss Brent's wool was inside the seat.

So now there were three people, all very frightened - and one of them had a gun! Blore came up to the house alone and I was ready with the clock. I saw Vera Claythorne shoot Lombard. Vera was afraid, but she was a strong young woman. Was she crazy enough by then to take her own life? She was. I was hiding in her room as she hanged herself. I picked up the chair and put it against the wall. I then found the gun at the top of the stairs. I was careful not to touch it.

And now?

I am going to put this letter in a bottle and throw the bottle from the island into the sea. At first I wanted my murders to be unsolvable. But in the end artists want people to enjoy their art. I want someone to know how clever I have been.

Perhaps, of course, the police have solved the mystery without my help. They have three important facts to help them:

1 The police know now that Seton really was a killer. So they know that one of the guests was <u>not</u> a murderer. So, strangely, that person was <u>the</u> murderer.

2 The line about the red herring in the poem should tell them something about Armstrong's death. Did Armstrong 'eat' the red herring, or did it eat him? Was he told lies and sent to his death?

3 There is the way in which I am now going to die. After I throw the bottle with this message into the sea, I am going to lie down with the weight of my body on my glasses. The glasses have **elastic** around them, tied to a gun, but not tightly. The elastic also goes around the key in the door. Then I will shoot myself, protecting my hand with a piece of cloth. As my hand falls to my side, the elastic will pull the gun towards the door. When it hits the door, the elastic will return to my glasses, below my body. When my body is found, the gun will be on the floor near the door. There will be a hole in my head, as my victims described.

When the sea is calmer, men and boats will come from the village. They will find ten dead bodies and a mystery on Soldier Island.

Lawrence Wargrave

elastic /ɪˈlæstɪk/ (n) something that becomes longer when you pull it. When you stop pulling it, it goes back to its usual size.

71

1 Work with two or three other students. Discuss the ten people on the island. Put them in order, from the worst criminal (1).

1	....	6	....
2	....	7	....
3	....	8	....
4	....	9	....
5	....	10	....

2 Discuss your list with another group. Explain your reasons. How much agreement is there between your lists?

3 In Chapter 6 Lombard says, 'There are crimes that nobody can punish you for. Old Wargrave, for example – his was a perfectly legal murder.' Discuss these questions.

> *Lombard saved himself, and not his men.*

> *Yes, but Marston forgot about the children that he killed!*

a Do you agree with him?

b Can you think of other 'perfectly legal' murders?

4 Imagine that you are on Soldier Island at the time of the murders. You realise that it is dangerous. Discuss these questions.

a Will you try to escape? How?

b Do you try to send a message to someone? How?

1 The police find a letter from one of the guests on the island. It is for the family of the victim, or victims, of his/her crime. In the letter, the criminal explains what happened and why. He/she is now very sorry. Write the letter.

2 Your class is now a court of law. Read your letter to the court. Does the court believe that the criminal is really sorry? What kind of punishment should that person get?

Work in pairs. Imagine that Soldier Island becomes famous after the murders. A group of business people decide to open the island to tourists. They ask you to do the planning.

1 Take a large piece of paper and prepare information for an Internet page. You should put on it:

- a map of the area, showing the island

- information about how to get there

- a short description of the island, and why it is famous

- a list of other places that are now on the island (for example, a children's playground)

- the opening hours of the house

Kill a Day on Murder Island!

2 You need to prepare for tours of the house before real visitors arrive. Have this conversation.

| Student A | You are playing the part of the tour guide. Imagine that you are taking a visitor around the house. Tell him/her what happened in each room. |

| Student B | You are playing the part of a visitor. Listen to the tour guide and ask a lot of questions. |

3 **You need to read about other places that are famous for murder.**

a Which of these two places do you think that visitors prefer to visit? Why? Will a different type of visitor be interested in the other place?

b Do you know of any other places that are famous for murder or for murderers?

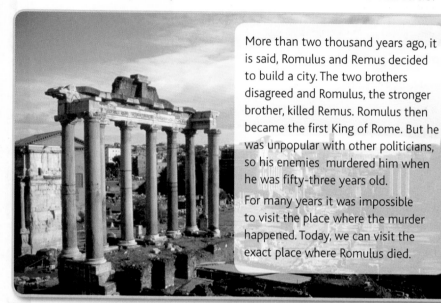

More than two thousand years ago, it is said, Romulus and Remus decided to build a city. The two brothers disagreed and Romulus, the stronger brother, killed Remus. Romulus then became the first King of Rome. But he was unpopular with other politicians, so his enemies murdered him when he was fifty-three years old.

For many years it was impossible to visit the place where the murder happened. Today, we can visit the exact place where Romulus died.

Alcatraz is a small island off the coast of San Francisco – the perfect place for a prison for dangerous criminals. The rocky island was very difficult to escape from. Some prisoners tried to swim across the sea, but they all drowned. For years, Alcatraz was home to some of America's most famous criminals, like Al Capone and George "Machine Gun" Kelly.

The last prisoners left in 1963, and today the island is a National Park. Every day, hundreds of visitors take the boat to Alcatraz.

4 You have discovered through your reading that tourists like waxworks. The owners of Soldier Island have agreed to fill a room with waxworks of famous real or fictional murderers. Make a list of ten well-known murderers. Then choose one and find information about that person on the Internet. Write about that person, giving reasons for a waxwork. Then present your idea to other pairs of students. Do they agree?